Stuart Lowes was born in the 1960's, an artist and a writer, he is also a northerner, he spent the first part of his life living in Byker, Newcastle, Gateshead and Sunderland, and for the last few years he has lived in Hertfordshire in Welwyn Garden City with his wife and children.

He has painted many portraits of many stars of stage and screen, including the queen, prince Phillip, king Charles Johnny Cash, Sir Cliff Richard, Neil Diamond, Elvis Presley, Michael Caine and many others.

Copyright c Stuart Lowes 2024

The right of Stuart Lowes to be identified as the author of this work has been asserted by the author in accordance with section 77 and 78 of the copyright, Designs and Patents act 1988. All rights reserved, no part of this publication may be reproduced, stored in a retrieval system or transmitted in any form or by any means, electronic, mechanical, photocopying, recording or otherwise, without the prior permission of the author.

Any person who commits any unauthorised act in relation to this publication may be liable to criminal prosecution and civil claims for damages.

This is a work of what the people mentioned in the book perceive as fact.

This is a biography.

Lowesstuart2@gmail.com

First published in 2024

Amazon book publishing.

<u>Stuart Lowes</u>

Dickie Pride

Croydon's Sheik, of Shake.

'The First'

'Slippin'n'Slidin'

Amazon

**Dickie Pride
Croydon's
Sheik, of shake.
'The First'
'Slippin n Slidin'
By
Stuart Lowes**

For Dickie

This book is dedicated to my wife and children who have had to put up with 'Dickie this, and 'Dickie that' etc. for the last few years

First Published in Great Britain
In 2025 by ASL

Copyright Stuart Lowes

All rights reserved, no part of this book can be stored reproduced or transmitted in any way or by any means electronic, mechanical Photocopying etc. Without the permission of the author

Except by a reviewer who may wish to quote brief passages for the purpose of a review

For more information NUMBER 2 AL7 3NZ.

Lowesstuart2@gmail.com

DICKIE PRIDE,
CROYDON'S SHIEK, OF SHAKE,
'The First'

'Slippin 'n' Slidin'.

This story is about Dickie Pride, the Rock and Roll performer who was a member of the Legendary Larry Parnes stable of Stars.

this group of people consisted of some Wonderful names that had been rechristened by pop impresario Larry Parnes, such as Marty Wilde, Vince Eager, Tommy Steele, Johnny Gentle, Duffy Power, and Billy Fury and various others, (no one knows what he was thinking with Julian X,) and now Dickie

Pride. (Richard Kneller) (Joe Brown categorically refused to be called Elmer Twitch, rightfully and wisely so).

Dickie's story was a tragedy, as it could have happened to any of our great stars of today, and nearly did to Elton John, who without the help and support of his doctors (and today's medical practices) and friends, he would not have survived to carry on with such a brilliant career,

The First as referred to in the book's title refers to the fact that Dickie was the first celebrity to die from a drugs overdose, making him instantly into a member of the infamous 27 club, those stars who have died over the years at the age of 27.

This was not the case with Dickie Pride, his story occurred in the late 1950's and the 1960's, a time when things were not as sophisticated medically as they are today,

the medical profession had very different ways of dealing with mental problems and ultimately did nothing to help Dickie Pride.

Dickie Pride is widely acclaimed amongst his peers as one of Britain's greatest rock and roll finds, who could have been one of our biggest stars and his career could have been astronomical on par with that of Sir Cliff Richard but that was not to be, maybe if it had been handled properly it would have been a different story, but because of his mental problems and the exploitation by his management,

namely that of Larry Parnes his career and ultimately his life, was cut short.

Dickie may have had mental problems that were handled very badly, but his manager was a manipulating man with too much power that he used to full advantage to his own ends.

you will see as the story of Dickie's life unfolds, that in my opinion one of the greatest assets to Dickie would have been a manager who was a father figure, that he could look up to and who would have guided him in his career and his life,

but no, unluckily he had to be stuck with Larry Parnes.

Vince Eager Said,

"He was totally different to the rest of us, and I think that had he been with another manager I think with someone who had a good strong fatherly instinct and control over Dickie, Dickie would have been one of the biggest stars this country had ever seen".

This is not the story of a young rock and rollers self-indulgence, who got what he deserved,

no Dickie had real mental health problems, that today would have been effectively dealt with by psychiatrists and drugs,

but in the 1960's it meant cutting away part of his brain.

Dickie was dynamite, his voice was one of the best in the music business at that time,

and by rights he could have been one of Britain's biggest stars, if it wasn't for his self-destructive personality.

Dickie Pride was born during the war years on October 21st, 1941.

at 74 Parchmore road, Thornton Heath, Croydon, to Frederick Charles Kneller a cockney and to Sarah Beatrice Kneller (nee Thomas) known as Beattie to her friends, she was Welsh.

Richard was born at home, like most people were in those days; it was unusual for a person to be born in hospital unless it was absolutely necessary.

Richard Charles Kneller's family was his father Fred, his mother Beatrice (Beattie), his older brother Robert, and his older sister Ann.

As it was the war years, it was not unusual for families to make their own entertainment by singing around the piano, acting out sketches and various other activities,

it was here that Richard could be found singing his heart out for his family and friends.

His mum Beatrice was a great singer who had a lovely voice, she was a member and mainstay of the local church choir and who used to visit the local old people's home for sing songs and concerts.

In Croydon, Heathfield vale,

there was a great sense of community spirit, and people genuinely helped each other,

they were glad for each other when anything good happened and felt equally bad when something bad happened.

as it was during the war years, Richard's father was in the Royal Engineers, and he was working as a machine operator.

he also suffered from Emphysema which was to plague him in his later life after the war, eventually resulting in his death when Richard was 15,

he was at that time due to leave school, but when his dad died, life in the Kneller household 'stopped for a while'.

Richard would become very distressed when his dad had an attack, Richard would be very disturbed, would panic and run from the room.

Richard was their second son; Richards's older brother was called Robert.

Richard was a healthy baby and a healthy child who from the moment he could talk he liked to sing.

Members of his family remember him at the age of three standing on the kitchen table at family gatherings singing to the assembled family, reciting Cockney rhymes,

which could be fairly saucy, which were taught to him by his dad Fred, who thought it was highly hysterical

(Fred was a proper Eastender so he knew all the oldies but goodies),

Mrs. Kneller was very proud of her son Richard and his talent and was known to spoil him,

especially in later years when his dad had died.

At the age of four Richard had an accident, he somehow managed to get his little finger chopped off with a pair of hedge trimmers, how he managed to do it is a bit of a mystery,

his sister Ann borrowed a pair of garden shears and was clipping the edge of the lawn with the set of garden shears when all of a sudden Richard's finger got in the way, he was rushed to hospital and had it stitched back on.

Richard was a normal kid who often got into fights, much to his mum Beatrice's annoyance, who being Welsh had a terrible temper and used to give Richard and his brother Robert a good tongue lashing for fighting, Richard could also speak a bit of Welsh,

they used to hang around a compound at the bottom of the street where workmen used to leave their tools while they were building the estate, this was the first council estate to be built after the war, it was called the compound because it was built by Italian prisoners of war who dug the drains for the estate.

Richard went to the Gilbert Scott primary school.

By the time Richard was eight he was a seasoned performer, performing in charity concerts.

He used to be a member of the Hill toppers youth club in Overbury crescent, New Addington.

Richard was also in the boy's brigade and was remembered for playing a trumpet up and down the street,

when Richard was a child, he nearly got stabbed to death as one bonfire night he was dressed up as a guy because he was the smallest and a drunk stabbed the guy, luckily missing Richard.
everyone who heard Richard or knew him knew

of his interest in music, so he was encouraged to play music and to sing,

he was also known for singing on the street corners, he used to call for one of the girls that he hung around with, who used to live on the same street as him, one of his first girlfriends, Thelma Dance by singing

'When I'm Calling You'. He used to do impromptu duets with Thelma; she had a voice like Doris Day,

Richard had a quirky smile; he was always laughing, and he liked to be liked.

In 1951, Richard won a scholarship to the Royal School of Church Music at Addington place, Croydon,

Which he took up partly through the prompting of his mother.

Richard was about 10 years of age,

Richard benefited greatly from his education, he was taught how to play various instruments and to read and write music,

he was able to play a wide range of instruments, including the piano and the drums, and his voice was trained.

While there the choirmaster Edward Wright took the choir to sing at Canterbury Cathedral in front of the Archbishop of Canterbury,

his tutors were so impressed with his voice that they were of the opinion that when his voice matured his voice would be extremely fine and would have an operatic tone.

There is a picture somewhere at the school of Richard with the archbishop of Canterbury.

When he was thirteen, he and his friends used to go carol singing at Christmastime,

he was often invited into people's front rooms to sing, by doing this he earned lots of money.

When Richard was fourteen, he performed at his cousins wedding and kept everyone entertained for hours with his songs and his wit,

When Bill Haley Topped the charts with Rock around the clock in 1956 Richards Father Died, a major turning point in his life, it has been said that his dad's death may have been behind Richard's problems,

Richard's sister Anne Parsons said

"Fifteen for a boy is just when you need a father's guidance and that is when he lost it".

And that 'everything stopped' for a while after that, she said 'that it was difficult for her to understand what happened to Richard even in the light of his father's early death, Richard was a beautiful child with blue eyes, curly hair and he had this lovely singing voice as well

'He was loved by everyone who met him, we were never well off, but who was in those days, but he never even had a very insecure childhood'

His Sister Also says that it annoyed her as a child that Richard was the centre of his mother's attention and when people came to the house, they all had to be quiet while his mother got Richard to sing. I used to think

"Let him sing if he wants, but why do the rest of us have to be quiet?" Whenever there was a family gathering, he would be strutted out to do his stuff and he did have a lovely voice he loved performing he loved being the centre of attention'.

Richard's singing career had scarcely registered on his sister's life, and she resented it when he became famous , people introduced her as Dickie Pride's sister.

She said that

she was annoyed with Richard, as she called him because she felt that he wasted so much of his time and in the end, his life'.

She said that she resented the way her mother pandered to his every whim when he became a star

'The only vegetable he would eat was frozen peas if he came home and there wasn't any, she'd have her coat on and she's be off down the shops, perhaps she could see that he needed to be looked after and cushioned, from life, which I couldn't see as his sister , After Richard went off to be a star we hardly saw him until he turned up in deep trouble with drugs with a great long beard and long hair'.

Richard 's Girlfriend Mandy said that 'everything was over the top when Dicks dad died, it was a pretty traumatic time'.

Because of this Richard was in shock and was prone to outbursts of temper, because of these outbursts of temper he was seen as a nutter.

Richard left the church school, his voice broke, it was a place for choristers, once your voice broke you had to leave,

Richard was a senior choirboy, one of the best (he was also asked to leave for playing around)

and he then went to the John Newnham School, Selsdon park road, South Croydon.

he was well known by this time for being able to sing a near perfect impersonation of Johnny Ray and was to be found drawing large crowds of friends and fans singing in the washrooms where the resonance of the porcelain from the toilets helped his performance,

he sang 'Cry', 'The Little White Cloud That cried', and' look Homeward, Angel' he won a talent contest with his impersonation of Johnny Ray.

While at the school he formed a skiffle group with some of his friends. They called themselves 'the Semi-tones'.

the actual events are that David Constable who played tea chest Bass, that he had made and his friend Roy Belcher on piano and his brother Tony who played the guitar, started a band,

they were fifteen, they were booked to play at the Westerham Coffee Bar to the crowd of customers,

they played for free as it gave them valuable experience of playing in front of an audience.

They were approached by Ron Sayer who played the piano,

who had heard them play at St Peters Church youth group, with his friend Dickie Kneller, they asked if they wanted to join their musical talents and form a band.

they were Roy o Brian on Bass,

Ron Sayer on piano,(Dickie's cousin)

Dave Constable on drums,

Roy Belsher on Sax,

Tony Belsher on guitar and Peter Weir,

they built up Quiet a large following, they first started at the Addington Hotel,

where Richard used to perform by himself with the resident house band, which at the time was run by a Jewish family,

The band took on a manager called Stuart Taylor, who used to drive them around,

They were called Dickie Sayer and the Semi tones,

Consequently, the band had three saxophone players at one time which created a nice fat sound, through these connections they were asked to play a Gig at the Café' Roche, where they played from ten at night till two in the morning,

they were allowed to play anything that they wanted to, except they had to play a song during the evening called 'My Yiddish Mama' for the management.

It was while they were working at the Addington hotel that they used to rehearse at a recording studio which was owned by Joseph Addad.

1957

The Kray twins
Television trial
Leaving school

Stuart managed to get Dickie and 'the Semi-tones' a gig at a club in East Ham, the two managers were so impressed with them that the band were introduced to them, they were Ronnie and Reggie Kray.

The Band did a Television trial for an Experimental television show on the lines of 6-

five special and Oh Boy for the producer Stuart Morris,

the show was to be called 'The Wind Machine Show'.

While they were trying to get a recording contract the band were to try out at Abbey Road studios,

which they found amusing as a new wooden floor had just been laid and the guys couldn't get right into their act in case they scratched the floors.

When Richard left school in 1957, the headmaster of the school Mr Myers, who was a great fan of Richard, and his wonderful singing voice,

as he had been a member of the schools Christmas choir, he took him around to each classroom to say goodbye and to sing to them, Richard sang 'Oh what a night' by Johnny Ray to each class.

In 1997 the John Newnham school association had a great tribute to their former pupil in their school magazine,

When Dickie left school, he kept the band going, he also worked on a variety of low paid labouring jobs,

One of them was as a Labourer on a council building site,

while working as a labourer he used to sing to his workmates, it wasn't unusual for Richard to serenade girls that he liked, he even serenaded one in Addington Park.

his friend Trevor Ure recalls

' I had sat next to him on the number 64 bus when we were returning from work, he said "Don't sit too close Trev"

I asked why and he pointed to his black shinny wellies, "I've just painted them " he said, I moved my new grey suit Slightly sideways,

he also worked as a car sprayer, and a stone masons assistant who specialized in making gravestones, He was fired from this job for being too cheerful and singing at work.

He worked as an electric plater and a lorry drivers' mate.

He used to rehearse his singing while traveling on the underground trains and buses to work,

Although he worked for a living all he really wanted to do was sing though.

He also got a job as an undertaker for three pounds a week but was sacked for skylarking.

On his 17th birthday he got engaged to his girlfriend Madeleine Jocelyn or Mandy as she was called,

she loyally toured the pubs and clubs with Richard, they had been girlfriend and boyfriend for years on and off,

she also dutifully sat while Richard performed,

and was still there when he did the Oh Boy Shows,

She said, that:

' in Croydon there is Surrey Street Market and the boys down there were tough, they became Dickies bodyguards which was really quiet strange they were big tough guys, this all happened because Dickie was a singer and a bloody good one as well'.

She was Richard's First serious girlfriend and for a time the most important person in Richard's life they had been going out together when they were both sixteen and their relationship is still an important part of her life,

you never forget your first serious boyfriend or girlfriend.

Their relationship was extremely intense she said that :

'Deep down he always knew that he would be a singing star someday he never rehearsed much and never really got nervous except for Oh Boy'.

Within six months of splitting up they both married other people, he tried to sabotage her wedding by getting married as well,

thereby preventing his sister from attending her wedding and she would have to turn up at his, his sister and Mandy were the best of friends and Richard had found out that she was getting married on St Patricks day from his mother,

but he couldn't get the special licence, so he had to get married a couple of days later,

they both married on the rebound to get at each other.

She Said 'he could sing any kind of music Jazz, choral, pop and was a great fan of Ella Fitzgerald and Mel Torme, particularly Fitzgerald's who's phrasing he tried to imitate

' 'He was a gentle man, fun loving always laughing and with a ready smile, he had a sympathetic and enquiring mind, he was an intelligent man there is no doubt about that,

but eventually he became someone I didn't know'.

it was at this time Richard was to record a demo disc which was paid for by a group of his friends, it is thought that one of the tracks was 'Such A Night' as he was very fond of impersonating Johnny Ray and Little Richard. And 'I Go Ape.

He also used to perform anything by Paul Anka.

1958

Larry Parnes
Dickie Pride
£15 a week

Two weeks after his 17th birthday in 1958 (about 4TH November) Richard by this time was performing in pubs, in and around Croydon and Tooting with his band the Semi-tones,

such as the Elephant and Castle where he performed regularly for two nights a week and at the Castle Pub in Tooting. On a Sunday.

The band won this regular slot by appearing in a talent contest, and won it,

they were offered a residency which they accepted,

the residency consisted of them working Monday nights, Thursday nights, Friday nights and Sunday morning.

The Castle Pub was a starting out venue where rock and roll acts would perform when they were first starting in the music business,

people like Marty Wilde, Tommy Steele etc.

and it still is today.

They did a couple of auditions at the Lime grove and Riverside Studios, but nothing came of them.

The official version of events says that Russ Conway the performer, dropped into the Union

Tavern in Tooting, for a drink on the way back from a date in Brighton.

Saw Richard perform his now established act, he was so impressed by his performance that he told his friend Larry Parnes about the young Slim, dark, blue eyed lad that he had seen.

Larry Parnes was an established manager and producer of Rock and Roll performers,

at this time, he was steering the careers of Tommy Steele, Marty Wilde, Billy Fury, Vince Eager and various other performers.

Larry Parnes who turned up with his friends Lionel Bart along with Russ Conway was impressed by Richard's performance.

this of course was not the real story,

what really happened was that while the band were performing at the Union Tavern in Tooting, Ron Sayer was approached in the toilets by Russ Conway who said that he was impressed by the band and wanted to know where they would be on Friday night as he wanted to bring someone along to see them,

so, on the Friday night they were to see the band at The Castle at 38 tooting high street SW17 ORG. Tooting.

Ron Sayer had a word with the manager of the pub and told him that he expected Russ Conway and some others to turn up,

but they couldn't turn up until late,

could he keep the bar open until they had been, the bar manager said that he would stay open until a quarter to eleven at the latest,

bearing in mind that closing time was ten thirty in those days and the Police were pretty strict then,

at 25 to 11 in walked Russ Conway, Trevor Peacock who was a songwriter in those days, Larry Parnes and Jack Good.

Russ told the Playwright Charles Langley:

"I dropped into a pub in Tooting and there was this incredible singer, I'd no idea who he was, but I was so impressed I talked to Larry Parnes about him, we went to see him the next week and took Lionel Bart with us. We were all so impressed that Larry decided to sign him 'on the spot'.

On Russ Conway's insistence he was included in a charity show that he was performing in at the Gaumont State in Kilburn, which was the biggest cinema in the country (now a bingo hall) and Larry Parnes was producing, Richard was just seventeen.

This version of events is a part fabrication, probably Fabricated by Larry Parnes to give the impression to the newspapers that he could spot talent, or to make his discovery more dramatic for the newspapers,

When he was introduced by the compare for the night Vince Eager,

he was introduced as Dickie because Vince realized as he was introducing him that he did not know his full name.

Richard went down a storm.

The record mirror wrote :

'He shook the building to the foundations, and he ripped it up from the start'.

It was Richards's first major public appearance. On the bill were more experienced Acts such as Marty Wilde, Vince Eager and Craig Douglas, Richard was a performer who had natural stage presence and was a first-class performer right from the start.

Larry Parnes who was watching from the wing's backstage was so impressed that he signed him immediately, as one of his stable of Performers. Not bad considering that Richard had never sang on such a large professional stage before. This is also partly fabrication Dickie's mother had to sign his contract because Dickie was still a minor and too young,

Richard, {now rechristened Dickie Pride by Larry Parnes as he did with most of his performers, i.e. Fury, Power, Pride, X etc., supposedly encapsulating their personality}, signed a four-year contract with Larry Parnes Starting at £15 per week increasing yearly over the next four years guaranteeing him £60 a week in the fourth year.

Parnes reneged on nearly all his contracts with his stars.

he never kept them on until their fourth year,

So, the promise of £60 by the fourth year was rubbish.

His contracts were so tightly drawn up that Parnes could do practically anything he wanted to do with his stars and get away with it.

One story about Parnes and one of his performers called Vince Eager explains a bit about this.

Vince Eager asked Parnes one day what had happened to his record royalties, which he had not received

"you're not entitled to any",

Parnes said to him,

"but it's in my contract that I am "said Vince Eager,

"It also says that I have power of attorney over you, and I say you're not getting any',

Vince was furious, his only option was to go to a solicitor, which he did, the contract was watertight,

the only thing that Eager could do was to refuse to work for the remainder of the contract, which was four years,

This is what he did he had to.

Vince was once offered a part in a movie by Burt Lancaster, but when Vince rang Larry to tell him about it, Larry was furious, he sent his driver to pick Vince up and to take him right home, he wanted Burt Lancaster nowhere near Vince because he thought that he wanted to have his wicked way with him; Larry had already tried and failed. (Burt Lancaster was supposed to have been Gay but there is no evidence that he was Gay and had supposedly kept it hidden for quite a few years).

Billy Fury fared a bit better than Vince Eager in the fact that he wrote his own songs,

as Billy Fury he was screwed, so his song writing name was changed to Wilbur Wilberforce on any of the songs that Billy wrote, and Parnes couldn't do anything about it, and more importantly he couldn't get any of the Royalties that Billy would be paid for writing the songs.

When Johnny Gentle's singles failed to reach the chart Larry Parnes just terminated his contract, as he did with Vince Eager, Duffy Power, Julian X, Sally Kelly and Dickie Pride. And to some extent Billy Fury,

when he wasn't making enough money for him.

Parnes was a con artist when he wanted to be,

Because he fancied him Larry Parnes managed to talk Johnny Gentle into signing with him, Johnny was a carpenter when he was 'found' by Parnes, his audition consisted of him singing along to a Marty Wilde record in Parnes' office,

he was then sent for a recording test, if he passed that he would be offered a three-year contract.

"I read through it briefly, but it was all legal jargon to me, and I couldn't make sense of it.

I seem to remember backing out a bit because I wasn't happy with the salary, I think it was £15 a week and I was getting £16 as a carpenter on my last job, and you know I hesitated a bit, knowing really that I would sign it anyway, but I hesitated, to show a little bit of resistance, hoping that he would put up the £15 a wee bit".

but he said

'Well, if you don't sign it you won't get your record contract, Phillips won't sign you unless you are managed by me',

so that was that I just signed, I thought not only would I not be getting signed by the biggest manager at the time,

but I'll lose my recording contract as well, or so he said".

The appeal for most artists to be with Parnes was that he could quiet literally take someone of the street and if they had an ounce of talent, he could make something of them, so most of his performers listened to what he had to say because they were under the impression that he knew best,

Dickie would sing what he was told to sing,

Whereas Billy Fury would say that he wouldn't sing this or that,

At first Dickie would sing what he was told to, but not always, sometimes he would tell Parnes if he thought a song was crap or not. Parnes often got the hump.

But let's face it Larry Parnes held Dickie back.

As the average weekly wage for an adult man was about £7. 10 shillings a week,

this deal seemed to be a fairly good deal. Especially for someone who was only seventeen years of age.

Margaret Simmonds first went out with Dickie when she was 15 they started dating in 1958, She was given a copy of Dickie's single, Slippin 'n' Slidin, but she stopped dating Dickie, and called it off because he was always going to the studio and she wanted someone who wanted to settle down and have a family, which she didn't think Dickie would do, because he was so involved with his music,

When she found out about Dickie's death she said

38

'It was such a waste from someone who was so talented and so young just twenty-seven.'

Sometime in 1958 Dickie made an appearance at the Radio and Television exhibition at Olympia in London.

1959

Slippin 'n' Slidin
Columbia records
Oh Boy
Primrose Lane

Richard or as he was now called Dickie Pride, he'd been rechristened that by Larry Parnes who had decided to drop the Kneller part of Richard name and he rechristened him, Dickie Pride which he had a habit of doing with nearly all of his 'stars' started performing regularly for Larry Parnes, touring and performing one night shows, he developed his legendary shake routine,

where he would shake uncontrollably as if he was having a fit.

His body shaking and vibrating at 200 shakes a minute, while he sang his song 'Slippin 'n' Slidin'.

He had then become known as 'the sheik of shake',

what was not known at the time was that every spasm of shaking caused him a lot of pain,

as he had a stomach ulcer, which was blamed on the irregular hours and irregular meals

and in his words 'and the fact that I'm really a frail sort of lad', an ulcer at Eighteen'.

Dickie was on the road so much that he would miss his girlfriend Mandy,

he used to ring her up when she was working as a telephonist,

from a public phone box and sing to her, she'd let the other girls listen to him singing his heart out.

Dickie now had a newly signed recording contract with Columbia Records, he had no problem securing a recording contract with

EMI's Columbia Records label. So with a new name so, it was into the studio to record his first single for Columbia Records 'Slippin 'N' Slidin' and for the B side 'Don't Make Me Love You', both brilliant,

with sales boosted by his dynamic stage performance of this song and his appearance on the Oh Boy shows, his performance can be seen on the only surviving episodes of this show that can be found for sale on eBay.

where Dickie can be seen standing stock still in front of the camera, because cameras in those days were so heavy, that they were not very manoeuvrable,

he can be seen performing 'Slippin 'N' Slidin' and from this footage it can still be seen how good he really was as a performer.

The Single Slippin 'n' Slidin was released twice,

the second time the B Side was Fabulous Cure to make the most of his appearance on Oh Boy.

Dickie's stage presence was obvious to everyone,

 Dickie was shy but completely potty on stage, he was also an education to the other performers, his act was dynamic, and it was the only act that other performers would watch and copy, he should have had a hit song,

but one of Parnes 'failings as a manager was that he couldn't pick a hit song if it slapped him in his face.

So, most of his stables of stars were lucky if they had gotten a good song.

It took Billy Fury three years to get a good hit song into the top ten, under Larry Parnes.

On May the 9th Dickie made an appearance on the Saturday club with Johnny Wiltshire and the Treble tones, Billy Fury, Group One, the ken Jones five, the Lennie Best Quartet with Elaine Delmar and Bert Courtney and the Wanderers.

then on the 30th of October 1959 Dickie's next record was released

Db. 4340, 'Primrose Lane' it was too sugary to be a rock and roll song and it only just made it into the top thirty,

at number 28,

and stayed there for just one week.

Despite also being released in three other countries as well, Germany, Netherlands and in Norway it was released on yellow vinyl.

42

Because there was so few good British rock and roll songs to go around,

Parnes concentrated his boys on covering American songs that had already been released in England by other performers,

sometimes Parnes' releases were in direct competition with their American counterparts, and for that matter other members of his stable also, with maybe two, three, or even four versions playing at one time all trying to outsell each other,

An example of this was Guy Mitchell's '*Singing the Blues*' and Tommy Steele's '*Singing the Blues*' both the same song with very little difference between the two of them

Or Billy Fury's '*it's Only Make Believe*'

and Conway Twitty's 'it's *Only Make Believe*'

so close that it's hard to distinguish one from the other.

This made it harder for any of Parnes' boys to score regularly in the charts.

Although Larry Parnes thought that Dickie was trouble,

Always thinking of the money that he was making, he was willing to keep Dickie on his books as long as possible as he was an attraction and a draw to his road shows.

People genuinely liked to see Dickie and he had lots of fans,

Larry thought that Dickie was a rebel, a non-conformist who wouldn't toe the line for Larry Parnes,

so, he was often on his back because of it.

Caught between the sheer physical pressures and as well as the Mental pressures of constant touring and being on the road,

recording television appearances and the lack of good songs that he wanted to sing,

Dickie began to develop genuine mental health problems, which were not helped by the drugs that he was now starting to abuse.

Dickie had an advantage over the rest of Parnes' performers as he had been educated at a music college and while there, he had learnt how to read music,

although there is no evidence that he actually wrote any music,

and he could play many musical instruments including the piano, the guitar, drums and the cornet, it was expected that by rights he couldn't fail.

He Appeared on the 'Oh Boy' show and was thought of as someone who was reliable, according to Jack Good,

so, he was made a regular between February 1959 and May 1959.

Marty Wilde said

"Jack Good used Dickie because he was the right sound and the right kind of voice what he wanted, I'm glad he used him and I'm glad that piece of film of 3 cool cats survived,

it's just lovely to see us all again as we used to be, Dickie was a great guy to work with

he had something that I thought some of us didn't have, a really good voice.

technically he was a good singer he loved Rock 'n' Roll obviously,

he used to do a lot of Little Richard type songs that were really very hard on the throat, he was a beautiful ballad singer, I always thought he was a cut above us in many ways.

A friend of Richard's called Trevor Ure said that he remember Dickie at the time he was doing the Oh Boy rehearsals, this was the days of pin stripe suits and bowler hats and The Times newspaper; I well remember him saying,

" I've got a great number this week Trev, it's called 'I Go Ape"

then he opened his brief case and produced a song sheet, he'd sing it with great power, complete with his typical shaking and finger clicking, the men in the carriage's faces were peering around the edge of The Times were a picture of astonishment and disbelief mingled with horror'.

Oh Boy was a very fast frantic nonstop show aimed at teenagers.

it had about 17 songs crammed into half an hour, Dickie Appeared on the show eight times,

which was transmitted live every Saturday night at 6pm.

The eight shows that Dickie appeared in were:

28 February 1959

the other performers on the show were, Jimmy Henney, Marty Wilde, Lord Rockingham's X1,

Cherry Wainer, Cuddly Dudley, Bill Forbes, The Dallas Boys, Mike Preston, Neville Taylor and the Cutters, Red Price, The Vernon Girls and Tony Sheridan. Dickie Sang 'Slippin 'N' Slidin'.

04 April 1959

The other performers on the show were, Tony Hall, Cherry Wainer, Don Lang, Lord Rockingham's X1, Neville Taylor and the cutters, Mike Preston, Lorrie Mann, Red Price, The Vernon Girls, Tony Sheridan, Chris Andrews, and Dean Webb.

And the special guest for this show was 'little miss dynamite 'Brenda Lee who sang 'Humming the Blues over you'

and she closed the show with

'Won't You Come Home Bill Bailey',

Dickie sang 'Slippin 'N' Slidin'.

11 April 1959

The other performers on the show were, Jimmy Henney, The Vernon Girls, Lord Rockingham's X1, Marty Wilde, Cuddly Dudley, Cherry

Wainer, The Dallas boys, Pierce Rodgers, Lorrie Mann, Bill Forbes and Red Price.

18 April 1959

The other performers on the show were, Tony Hall, The Ink Spots, Lonnie Donegan and his skiffle group, Cherry Wainer, The Vernon Girls, The Dallas Boys, Neville Taylor and the Cutters, Lorrie Mann, Pierce Rogers, Tony Sheridan, and Jack Goods Lord Rockingham's X1.

25 April 1959

The other performers on the show were, Jimmy Henney, Don Lang, Bill Forbes, Billy Fury, Cuddly Dudley, and Michael Cox, the Dallas boys, the Cutters, Nicky Martin, the Vernon Girls, Red Price and Jack Good's Lord Rockingham's X1.

Dickie sang Long Tall Sally accompanied by Lord Rockingham's X1 Dickie also sang'

Come Softly to me 'accompanied by Jean and Margaret, 'Cool Shake' and 'Long Tall Sally'.

09 May 1959

The other performers on the show were, Jimmy Henney, Conway Twitty, Marty Wilde, Cherry Wainer, and Billy Fury Cuddly Dudley. the Dallas Boys, Tony Sheridan and the Wreckers, Maureen Kershaw, The Vernon Girls, Lord Rockingham's X1, Red Price and Dean Webb.

23 May 1959

The other performers on the show were, Jimmy Henney, Renee Martez, Cliff Richard, Marty Wilde, Red Price, The Dallas Boys, Cherry Wainer, Billy Fury, Bill Forbes, Lord Rockingham's X1, Terry White and The Vernon Girls.

30 May 1959

the other performers on the show were, Tony Hall, Jimmy Henney, Cliff Richard and the drifters (the Shadows to be), Marty Wilde, The Dallas Boys, Cherry Wainer, Lord Rockingham's X1, Don Lang, Red Price, The Vernon's Girls, Cuddly Dudley, Mike Preston, Neville Taylor and the Cutters, Peter Elliot, Billy Fury and Bill Forbes. Sang 'TV Hop' there are only two surviving shows in the archives of thirty episodes one from Saturday 4th of April 1959 and the other is the final show from the 30th May 1959 on the first show Dickie is seen singing an extended complete version of Slippin 'n' Slidin and on the one from the final show he is seen performing a short version of 'Slippin 'N' Slidin' of only one verse as Jack Good was attempting to cram in as many highlights of all the best songs in the series into this final show.

He is also seen singing 'Three Cool Cats' with Marty Wilde and Cliff Richard.

On June 13th Dickie made another appearance on the Saturday club with Jim Dale, Franklyn Boyd, Bob Court, the Lana sisters, the Treble tones, the Betty Smith quartet and the ken Jones Five.

Dickie spent the Summer at the Palace Theatre Blackpool as part of Harry Fielding's 2'30 specials program,

this show featured a lot of the Oh Boy cast including Marty Wilde, Cherry Wainer, Red Price, Mike Preston, Cuddly Dudley, Tony Sheridan and Sally Kelly.

Mandy was around at this time and at the time he did pub gigs as well, she said

'It was just like an ordinary job of work by then', and she would just sit around doing paperwork 'but when Dickie was on stage performing nothing else mattered to him,

 he was magnetic on stage, no one got up to go to the loo when Dickie was singing and he had a voice that would give you that little tingle up your spine, he had great charisma and stage presence,

 I just thought that it would go on like that forever. he would sing all the songs to me from the stage, just we two knew about that, but eventually he became someone I didn't know'.

They eventually broke up, partly due to his other girls,

 but mainly because the music became too important, she said ,

'Communication was difficult and breaking down, we had no phone,

I heard about him and other girls he had, I suppose I just grew up and thought I wouldn't have any more of it,

I think he also grew away from me,

perhaps he felt he didn't need me anymore; it was a tragedy because if I had been there, it would never have happened.

I was his friend more than anything else, that's what makes it sad, and he was so talented.

Later I met girls who had been out with him, and they said that when they were out with him, all he ever talked about was me'.

Dickie was handy with his fists, and this came in handy.

He was very protective of Mandy and if anyone so much as look at her,

Dickie became a bit of a target with some of the yobs who wanted to wind up the performers, he was often in trouble,

but not of his own doing, and occasionally he had the odd punch up with fans.

Dickie used to get heckled by some of the teddy boys,

but his general response was

'I'm getting paid for making a fool of myself, what's your excuse',

But it wasn't unusual for him to jump off stage for a fight,

 usually, he was the first to get the nut in,

On one occasion he threatened a whole theatre of fans and told them that he would see them all outside after the show,

 when he went outside after the show there was usually no-one there, as the audience had taken it in good stead and forgotten about it,

 but unluckily one night in Birmingham Dickie had threatened to take the whole of the audience on and when he got outside there was a large gang of mad Brummie Tearaways waiting to do him over,

that night he had to run for it, and he just managed to get away by the skin of his teeth,

 but Dickie still didn't learn,

 and the next time there was trouble he threatened to take everyone outside and give them all a good hiding.

They say hit first and talk afterwards, Dickie didn't talk at all, and he would just hit out and try from the start to lay you out.

 He used to get very jealous when anyone talked to Mandy his girlfriend, even when he was performing on stage, if he had been more famous, he may have got away with having a temper

but he wasn't famous enough so people wouldn't put up with it.

Larry Parnes hated having the girls around, he tried to keep the girlfriends away as much as possible,

and he was very rude to them, as he didn't want them around at all,

Dickie used to take offence when Larry was rude to Mandy,

Dickie and Larry used to clash with each other over this.

Dickie was not liked as a person by Larry Parnes and thought him too independent,

but Larry was good at spotting talent, even though he was crap at spotting good songs.

Duffy Power who worked with both Billy Fury and Dickie, and lived together in various rooms while on tour, said of Dickie

"Dickie was absolute magic on stage, completely spellbinding,

On tour Dickie got a bit jaded listening to the same people singing the same songs every night.

But Dickie was the singer that the others went to the wings to watch, you couldn't take your eyes of him'.

Georgie Fame who backed Dickie in the early days remembered

"If there was anyone in the audience heckling, he'd get off the stage and go and thump them".

He was also the man, who taught me to sing harmony, when I'd never even heard of it,

He got three or four of us together on the back of the coach singing and that's how I learnt to do it,

he was tremendously talented, and his death was a tragedy.

it was a funny sort of set up because although he was not that high up the bill,

he closed the first half of the show, which is like being second on the bill,

and he got extra songs to sing, so it was like Parnes recognized that he deserved a top billing but wouldn't give it to him,

But Parnes didn't want to give him the recognition he deserved,

Dickie would run up to the drums and play them, he would go to the piano and play that,

He would annoy other acts by doing this because they couldn't play anything,

he would get annoyed too because he had to work with some crap acts, some of the acts were terrible (if anyone has seen Jess Conrad's act, they will know what I mean}, but they were doing better than him because they were pretty boys,

and in those days, it was all about image, especially in the eyes of Larry Parnes who as it was rumoured was a homosexual man and took a liking to the pretty boys that he managed.

So, looks were very important to him and Dickie was not a pretty boy,

There was a lot of backbiting so that a person could get ahead, and a lot of pressure from your peers,

On top of this Dickie hated pop music and he called it Ricky – tic music,

he'd make a face and move his hand up and down with rhythm to show what he meant."

Dickie was even offered the part as buttons in the panto Cinderella,

but Larry wouldn't let him do it because he was filming for a television Documentary about the story of Rock and roll,

 and Dickie was needed for some of the filming about his stable of stars'.

When he started to make money, the first thing that Dickie did was to buy himself a car, in about 1959 (as did Billy Fury), he drove everywhere in his two seated red Sprite sports car,

during shows and afterwards he would take Gene Vincent for a quick spin Gene Vincent liked and respected Dickie, they spent many a night getting drunk together as they both liked whiskey.

The car became the bane of his neighbours, he managed to turn it over once in his street because he was driving it too fast.

Johnny Gentle was a friend of Dickie's and used to perform with him on some of the Parnes Package tours, he said about Dickie's car, when he, Duffy and Dickie were rushing to get home because they all had dates that night, it Conked out

"We pushed it to the nearest garage, but it was closed, we were settling down for the night which isn't easy three people trying to sleep in a two-seater,

When the Parnes coach passed us".

Hal Carter fared no better in Dickie's car he went for a drive once and swore he would never get in the car again.

As the car was low slung Dickie would drive it with the bonnet of the car directly under the back of the lorry at a very fast speed.

With the radiator about three feet away from the rear wheels,

Hal was terrified, he swears to this day that Dickie had a death wish.

Joe Brown Confirmed that Dickie was a mad driver,

he drove with him once and swears he would never do it again,

on that occasion a man stepped between Dickie's car and the one in front and Dickie closed the gap and trapped him.

He Also says that 'Dickie had a death wish

'He had a strong stage presence and tremendous talent he was the best of us all when it came to singing' ' if he could have kept his head,

he would have been very very famous

'Dickie Seems to have a death wish he kept picking fights with people three times the size of him.

At the Liverpool Empire someone hit Billy Fury, the police collared him, but Dickie attacked him even when the police were holding him'

He was our Michael Jackson more than anything else, he had so much talent it was awesome to behold,

and it was one of the great tragedies of British music that he couldn't hold it together'.

being a boisterous young lad he was prone to playing the odd practical joke, on one occasion after leaving school

and while he was doing the 'Oh Boy' shows in 1959,

Dickie, Billy Fury and Marty Wilde sat on the grass outside John Newman's school, and they had to be asked to leave by the headmaster as lessons in the school had totally seized up. Whilst the pupils watched them, from their classrooms.

 the three of them thought this was highly hilarious and were laughing as the three of them crammed into Dickie's tiny little sprite,

Dickie used to call Marty Wilde 'dad' whom he was very close to,

Marty used to call him 'son'. It was nothing to do with their ages but a reflection on their comparative heights.

Dickie was slated to play the artful dodger in the film Oliver, but he eventually grew too tall.

Dickie was smoking dope very early on in his career and popping pills, most of the young beat musicians did pills,

 not the ones that were hired from Jack Good, but the beat musicians,

 and were very much into drinking,

 which Dickie had a problem with right from the start,

 when he drank, he didn't just get drunk, he got unconscious, he couldn't hold his drink.

On April 17th, 1959, he was prone to temper outbursts and because of this he was arrested and appeared before the Kent Quarter sessions, for being drunk, and trying to break into a shop,

he smashed a shop window at West Wickham and for trying to take a motor scooter without the owner's consent.

He took it for a joyride and was caught by a policeman,

He pleaded guilty and was put on probation for three years.

The friend that was charged with him,

Brian Bentley who was a nineteen-year-old machine operator of Shepherds way South Croydon,

was also put on three years' probation,

Dickie said

"Mr. Parnes practically blew my head off when he heard I was in trouble, I'm feeling very very miserable, I had so much to drink for a start and I was with the wrong crowd,

but I know I did wrong and I'm not trying to blame anyone".

Lads being lads this was not too much to worry about as it were lads being lads,

because of the economic climate of the day though the daily newspapers were outraged. Totally blowing it out of proportion,

there was a public outcry resulting in questions being asked in the House of Commons

"Is this the kind of person that should be on National television?" (John Knight, Daily Sketch, April 24, 1959)

by this time, he had appeared on television in the show 'Oh Boy'.

This was typical of Dickie he was a young lad who was enjoying his life, so he was a joker,

On an early performance of Oh Boy that was recorded for television he can be clearly seen kissing one of the Dallas boys on the cheek, as they backed Bill Forbes while singing

'Cool, Cool, Water'

Georgie Fame Said I just joined Larry Parnes from my first professional gig with Rory Blackwell and The Black Jacks and Rory was known as Rory' Shakes 'Blackwell,

he used to do that, and Dickie got his shake from Rory Blackwell, my first boss, so, I knew the shake thing I didn't know anything about Dickie though,

'I enjoyed working and playing on stage with Dickie More than any of the other artists that includes Billy Fury,

including Gene Vincent,

Dickie had a long way to go but unfortunately, he cut it short'.

On June the 13th Dickie Appeared on Saturday Club with Jim Dale, Franklin Boyd, Bob Court, the Lana Sisters, the Treble tones, the Betty Smith Quintet and the Ken Jones Five.

During one of the Parnes tours, Hal Carter had to get Dickie and Billy Fury out of the police cells,

it was fashionable at the time for singers to wear cowboy boots, gun belts and 45's,

one day at a stop over at Grantham for a cup of tea Dickie and Billy went into a chip shop and said

"This is a stick up, give us some fish and chips "

Then they went into a restaurant and said

"This is a stick up, give us a table", they were just mucking about,

But the man in the chip shop phoned the police and told them he'd been held up by two cowboys,

the police arrested Dickie and Billy,

but Hal Carter managed to get them out of the cells the police realised it was just a bit of fun and they were released with a flee in their ear and with just a caution.

Dickie and Billy formed a very close friendship and one day they were spotted with identical cuts on their hands both self-inflicted,

they had cut their hands and rubbed their blood together and announced that they had sealed their friendship in blood

and that they were now blood brothers

Hal Carter said, Dickie used to play two shows a night even if tickets were sold or not,

at one place, in the audience there were six people in the theatre, it held about fifteen to sixteen hundred people

and there were six people in the audience on the Wednesday night, first house and Dickie who had a wicked sense of humour walked out and he did the first number, and they applauded and he said to the audience,

'Thank you very much I would like to say to you "if you stay for the whole of my act I'll get you a taxi to take you home after".

Georgie Fame said, 'Dickie had a wonderful sense of humour but he was wicked he got us into serious trouble once,

What happened we were on stage and Dickie had gone out for a pint in the pub between shows,

in those days we always wore a bit of make up on stage cos of the lights, we weren't usually allowed to wear it on a Sunday because of the lord's day observance society,

Dickie had gone to the pub and had gone in on his own with the makeup on and somebody said 'pufftа' and he whacked them, then he ran back into the theatre,

anyway, the show went on for a couple of hours, at the end of the concert we couldn't get out of the theatre, there were about two hundred local Birmingham Teddy Boys outside the stage door screaming for blood'.

Dickies Stage act was hypnotic and always went down a storm, but despite his constant touring to promote his music and frequent Television appearances his records although well received barely managed to break into the top twenty.

1960

Another tour.
Gene Vincent and Eddie Cochran.
Pride with Prejudice.

On January the 2nd, Dickie made a further appearance on the Saturday club with the Zodiacs, June Marlow, Dick Jordan, Bert Weedon Quartet, Ronnie Price Quartet and the Delaney Band.

Dickie Started another Parnes tour but the headliners on this 30-day tour they were two of America's greatest Rock and roll stars,
Eddie Cochran and Gene Vincent,

Which kicked off at The Gaumont Theatre in Ipswich on January 24th this was called 'The Fast – Moving Beat Show'

this tour consisted of some of England's finest rockers,

including Billy Fury, Duffy Power, Dickie, Vince Eager and various other performers.

This tour jumped across England to various places such as The Glasgow Empire, The Granada Woolwich then back to The De Montfort Hall in Leicester.

Dates were

24th January	Ipswich Gaumont
28thJanuary	Coventry Gaumont
29th January	Worcester Gaumont
30th January	Bradford Gaumont
1 - 6th February	Glasgow Empire
7th February	Sheffield Gaumont
13th February	Woolwich Granada
14th February	Taunton Gaumont
18th February	Leicester De Montford Hall
20th February	Dundee Caird Hall
21st February	Wembley Empire Pool

24th February	Stockton Globe
26th February	Cardiff Gaumont
29th February	Leeds Empire
1 - 5th March	Leeds Empire
7 - 12th March	Birmingham Hippodrome
14 - 19th March	Liverpool Empire
21 - 26th March	Newcastle Empire
28th March - 2nd April	Manchester Hippodrome
4 - 9th April	Finsbury Park Empire
11 - 14th April	Bristol Hippodrome
16th April	Bristol Hippodrome

On April 12th Dickie appeared on the royal Albert Hall in London for the BBC Light Program Big Beat Along with Adam Faith, Craig Douglas, Duffy Power, The John Barry 7, Bert Weedon Johnny Wiltshire, The Treble tones, Robin Rock Unit, David Ede, Lorrie Mann, Colin Day Ray Pilgrim and the compere was Brian Mathews

But Tragedy struck, Gene Vincent and Eddie Cochran were involved in a road accident, Gene

Vincent was badly injured but Eddie Cochran was so bad that he died of his injuries in hospital

When Eddie Cochran was in the accident that killed him on April the 17th it was Dickie, Billy Fury and Larry Parnes who were called to the hospital to see Eddie.

Parnes' comments to the press about Eddie's crash were not well received.

Within a couple of months of Eddie's death Larry Parnes cashed in on Eddie's misfortune, with an Eddie Cochran Tribute Show, it was called Larry Parnes presents a tribute to the late Eddie Cochran,

Held on Monday June 27th, 1960, at the Birmingham Hippodrome

All the acts had to perform one Eddie Cochran number each, he announced on the posters that he would donate a percentage of the evening's takings from the two shows one at 6-25 and one at 8-30 To Eddie's family

(it is unknown if he did, he didn't make a song and dance about it if he did, which in itself would have been unusual for Larry Parnes, but knowing Parnes it would have been as little as possible anyway).

Those appearing that night were Billy Fury, Joe Brown, Lance Fortune, Keith Kelly, Davey Jones, Georgie Fame Peter Wynne, Nero and His Gladiators, Billy Raymond, The Beat Boys and Julian. But not Dickie Pride.

Vince Eager had quit Parnes because he didn't agree with Parnes who was blatantly exploiting Eddie Cochran's death.

On April 23rd Dickie was booked to appear on Jack Good's new television show Wham!! Which was to replace Boy Meets Girl,

Dickie was held in such high esteem by Jack Good that he was asked to appear on the first show,

the ABC Weekend Show only lasted eight weeks from April 23rd till June it was filmed at the ABC Studios in Manchester and was hosted by Keith Fordyce,

Its premise was to introduce new talent every week with no fewer than eight stars appearing every week,

But it was pulled from the air with ABC Management saying in their statement

'There is no longer a viewing public for teenage rock 'n' roll type programs.

The Stars that appeared were Joe Brown, Jess Conrad, Billy Fury, The Vernon's girls, Danny Rivers,

Johnny Kidd, (Who started wearing his famous eye patch at one of these shows at the suggestion of Jack Good), Vince Taylor and Dickie Pride,

Dickie also made two more appearances on the show on Episode three on the 7th of May 1960

and his final appearance on the sixth show on 28th May 1960.

Jack Good tried his luck in America when the show was cancelled and produced a pilot for a show at his own expense (£20 000 of his own money) Called Shindig, it wasn't picked up by any of the television networks

But four years later in 1964 it was picked up in America and Jack Good was called back to produce it and it became one of America's most successful music shows.

After this tour it was back to the studio, but this time Dickie was to record his only album, for Columbia records,

on the day he was to record the album,

he was late arriving, so there was no time for a run through or time to rehearse.

The results were nonetheless very impressive, and everyone had to admit that Dickie's Voice was great,

and lamented the fact that if it wasn't for Dickie's temperament his voice could have carried him all the way to the top,

The album itself was wonderful,

the Album was called *'Pride without Prejudice'* named by Larry Parnes,

Dickie had been signed to Columbia by Norrie Paramor. And the Album was recorded with the Eric Jupp and his orchestra.

On the album he was able to record the type of music that he wanted to, by Cole Porter, Irving Berlin, George Gershwin and other great song writers,

but it was a mystery why Parnes didn't cash in on Dickie's Performance and let him sing more of this kind of music.

The New Musical Express' news editor was known to give musicians a very rough ride, if he took the fancy and was known as a Grice,

He had nothing but praise for Dickie's album saying

"The full range of talents and versatility is the keyword of this disc".

it seemed as if Dickie was being Manoeuvred into a more adult market,

just as Billy Fury was, and the decision to release Dickie's album with lots of ballads was just a way of jumping onto this bandwagon

as most of the Rock and Roll stars were now concentrating on ballads, over the last couple of years such as Cliff Richard and Elvis Presley.

Dickie's album was brilliant though and his voice was great, but the fickle record buying public were not buying records by the old school of Rock and Rollers,

they considered them dated and stuck in the 1950's, an old decade,

the public were buying records by the new stars like Del Shannon and John Leyton, so this album was not going to be a best seller unfortunately.

Dickie Appeared in summer season at the Great Yarmouth Britannia Theatre, opening July 24 with Billy Fury and the Beat boys,

Vince Eager and The Quiet Three, Johnny Gentle Keith Kelly Davy Jones and Julian X/

The compere was Phil G.

It was about this time that Dickie recorded a twenty-five-minute live broadcast for radio Luxembourg from a Slough ballroom with Marty Wilde's backing band the Wildcats,

they were loaned to him by Marty Wilde for this broadcast.

Dickie was booked to appear on the Parnes' Big Star Show, at the Liverpool Empire where he performed 'Ain't She Sweet'.

The Beatles, then the Silver Beatles were to be the backing band for some of the Parnes shows but Parnes changed his mind, and didn't book them.

as he thought that Dickie Pride and the Beatles would be too much trouble. Parnes failed to sign as the Beatles manager for a second time.

On September 24th he started another tour starting at the Slough Adelphi

Sept 25th   Woolwich Granada
Sept 27th   Maidstone Granada
Sept 28th   Bedford Granada

Sept 29th	Kettering Granada
Sept 30th	Grantham Granada
Oct 1st	Mansfield Granada
Oct 3rd	Rugby Granada
Oct 4th	Aylesbury Granada
Oct 5th	Dartford Granada
Oct 6th	Harrow Granada
Oct 7th	Free Trade Hall Manchester
Oct 8th	Tooting Granada
Oct 9th	Walthamstow Granada
Oct 11th	Kingston Granada
Oct 12th	Southend
Oct 13th	Edmonton
Oct 14th	Plymouth
Oct 15th	Taunton
Oct 16th	Preston
Oct 25th	Sheffield
Oct 26th	Derby
Oct 27th	Elephant and Castle
Oct 28th	Cardiff
Oct 29th	Cheltenham

Georgie Fame Says

'He genuinely loved jazz singing, and he obviously had a desire to do it,

but we were all locked into what we were doing with Parnes.

There was a Trad boom in 1960 and Larry Parnes Decided to jump on the band wagon, so he put a big band on stage and called it the Rock and Trad show, that gave people like Dickie an opportunity to move slightly into the jazz sound thing'.

Duffy Said

"Dickies voice had got this wonderful sad quality sort of resigned sadness in it,

if you know a bit about singing you can hear that, you know it's not found often,

it's a great thing to have if you've got that naturally, they all try to do it'.

It was like a very good knowing knowingness about it, for someone who was only eighteen,

The quality is there, and they all knew it, if he'd looked like Elvis, we'd have been more frightened. He would have been more dangerous; he wasn't a bad looking bloke, though he didn't look like one of the glamour boys like Billy Fury was.

it's interesting to note that in an interview in 1985 with Radio London, Paul Mc Cartney said that he had seen this show when he was 13,

and that it was Dickie's voice and performance that stood out that night and it was that performance that persuaded him to be a musician,

the Beatles recorded 'Ain't She Sweet' while they lived and performed in Germany.

In November He was on another Parnes tour Called Rock n Trad Spectacular, Idols on Parade, it's Producer Was Jack Good.

It started in Sunderland on the 1st

Nov 2nd	Hammersmith
Nov 4th	Bournemouth
Nov 5th	Ipswich
Nov 6th	Leeds Odeon
Nov 7th - 13th	Liverpool
Nov 14th -21st	Manchester
Nov 22nd	Romford Odeon

Nov 23rd	Rochester Gaumont
Nov 24th	Doncaster Gaumont
Nov 25th	Chester Gaumont
Nov 26th	Worcester Gaumont
Nov 27th	Bradford Gaumont
Nov 28th	Coventry Gaumont
Nov 29th	St Albans Odeon
Nov 30th	Dover ABC
Dec 1st	Llandudno Empire
Dec 2nd	Shrewsbury Granada
Dec 3rd	Cleethorpes Ritz
Dec 6th -11th	Newcastle Empire

Featuring Billy Fury, Joe Brown, Tommy Bruce, Nelson Keene, Peter Wynne, Red Price, The Valentine Girls and Jimmy Nichols and his New Orleans Rockers.

The first song he sang was

'Time and the River 'a big hit for Nat king Cole.

During 1960 there was a series of secret sessions where Dickie met up with Harry Robinson (Lord Rockingham) who was now a producer,

He had worked with Dickie on 'Oh Boy' At the live transmissions at the Hackney empire and were the house band, Lord Rockingham's X1,

These sessions were held at the Decca recording studios,

These sessions had to be held in secret as Dickie was a Columbia Records recording artist.

Jess Conrad was recording his single 'Cherry Pie' and was having real trouble reaching a certain note, so in stepped Dickie, as he had a trained voice, he had no problem reaching the note.

This wasn't the first time that Dickie had to do something like this; it was done again when Dickie appeared on the 'Wham' show for television,

Danny Rivers was having trouble reaching the high note on an Elvis Presley number (Such a Night?)

so once again in stepped Dickie, Coincidently Jess Conrad was also on the same show promoting 'Cherry Pie' so when it came to the notes Jess couldn't reach in stepped Dickie again, who sang the notes out of sight, backstage.

1961

Sacked

Probation

In February he was on another tour this time the promoters were the Stars of Saturday Club, starting at

        Chelmsford on Feb 19th

Feb 22nd   Lowestoft Theatre Royal

Feb 23rd   Tonbridge wells Assembly Rooms

Feb 24th   Worthing Pier Pavilion

Feb 25th   Trowbridge Gaumont

Feb 26th   Plymouth Odeon

And a second tour in February with the stars of Saturday club, Ricky Valance, Matt Monroe, Bert Weedon, Johnny Angel, Linda Doll, Peter Chester group, Bruno Martini group, Gene

Vincent, Chris Wayne, the Echoes, Julie Rayne and the compere was Sammy Samwell.

March 12th Dickie appeared at the Gaumont Ballroom, Bradford

And on March 18th another show at the Bradford Gaumont ballroom

Dickie, sick of performing rock and roll numbers, asked Larry Parnes if he could sing something more demanding, and more in tune with his voice, such as Gershwin, Rodgers and Hart and Cole Porter,

Parnes was having none of it, after all he wasn't in that side of the business, and wanted him to sing rock and roll he insisted that Dickie sing the same three rock songs every night, because that's how he made his money, insisting that Dickie sang the same three rock songs every night.

Dickie was furious.

It was well known that he and Parnes were not getting on well; he took this as a personal snub. Dickie decided that he was in a no-win situation and felt he was trapped in the Dickie pride persona he just wanted to be Richard Kneller and sing, sing the songs that he wanted to sing.

  Dickie's repertoire was pretty good too, he didn't sing Eddie Cochran because he toured with him and the memories were too much,

but he did sing a lot of Buddy Holly,

 his favourites songs were

'That'll Be the Day',

'Great Balls Of Fire', 'Long Tall Sally', Heartbreak Hotel,

 Nat king Cole's 'When I Fall in Love',

'Peggy Sue' and anything else by Buddy Holly

 He was a great fan of Ella Fitzgerald and used to try and imitate her phrasing

Dickie was a great drummer,

 on April 21st he performed at the Chippenham Corn Exchange with the Brook Brothers, and the Scorpions, during the sound check with the Scorpions, Dickie jumped on stage and proceeded to play the Drums,

 During that evening's performance he did it again and played the second set of drums that were on stage, the Scorpions were impressed, so they gave Dickie a lift home to Croydon.

Hal Carter who was Larry Parnes Road manager recalled

"Dealing with Dickie became more and more difficult he was a genius in my opinion but with a couple of flakes missing,

The trouble was that when you walked into a room you didn't know whether you were going to get the genius or the madman.

He had a tendency to hit out with his fists rather than talk,

the slightest frustration would start him swinging,

if he drank, he didn't just have a drink, he got legless,

and he was into smoking dope early on'.

When Dickie first met Duffy Power, he tried to make a show of who was the stronger of the two of them he tried to bully Duffy,

While Duffy was asleep on the coach Dickie tried to wind him up,

Duffy was having none of it he grabbed Dickie by the throat and pinned him against the window and Dickie said,

 'Alright Alright' and they were great friends after that.

The only problem Duffy had with Dickie was that Dickie would treat him like Rambo after that, Duffy couldn't go into transport cafes with him because he would get into fights and expect Duffy to be Rambo,

 with seven or eight truckers to argue with, he didn't want to be Rambo for Dickie.

Dickie was only a little fellow and wasn't very tall but according to Danny Rivers

"Dickie was well endowed: he used to say on the tour bus to the women on the tour

 'Cop a load of that',

 With him being such a little fella,

 but in height only".

Dickie worked with Marty Wilde, Cliff Richard on the Radio and Joe Brown,

 who is one of the most talented individuals to ever come out of the British Pop scene of the 50's and 60's, when Joe Brown was asked who was the most talented of all of Larry's boys

"Dickie Pride, definitely Dickie Pride he was the most talented of us all,

he was a great singer, ask any of the boys and they'll all say Dickie Pride, he had a strong stage presence and tremendous talent,

if he could have kept his head together, he would have been very, very famous.

I've no doubt about his talent, he was the best of all of us when it comes to singing, he was our Michael Jackson more than anything else,

he had so much talent it was awesome to behold, and it was one of the great tragedies of British music that he couldn't hold it together"

He also said that Dickie seemed to have a death wish as he kept picking fights with people three times his size.

Hal Carter Said, one day Larry said to me

"Go and sort out Dickie Pride"

Larry couldn't handle him anymore,

so I went off and virtually lived with him for a month.

I remember one night we ended up back at his mother's house in Croydon.

we had to share a room because it was only a small house,

and in the night, I was awoken by this extraordinary noise like an animal in pain,

it took me a bit to realize it was Dickie and when I pulled the curtains back a bit,

there was enough light to see that he was sitting bolt upright in bed making this weird noise and pulling at his face, I don't just mean pulling, it was almost like he was trying to tear his own face off,

but the strange thing was that he was still asleep.

I tried to stop him, but I couldn't, he was too strong, but eventually he settled down again and lay still, he'd been asleep the whole time.

At the time I didn't know what to make of it, although it's pretty obvious to me now that he was a deeply troubled young man, and this was one of the symptoms.

I've often thought about this incident since and the only explanation I can come up with is that he wasn't actually trying to tear off his face, what he was trying to do was tear off the mask we had put on him,

 he was trying to get out from behind the Dickie Pride mask and get back to being himself"

 According to Duffy Power, Dickie used to pull at his face when he was stressed.

In the morning, he couldn't remember anything about it.

 I would say that Dickie was a genius, he was a hell of a talent,

 he could sing anything, and he could dance, play piano, guitar, anything really,

I would say he was a genius with a couple of flakes missing,

 the trouble was he was completely violent and uncontrollable",

after a month of living with Dickie he had to admit defeat he couldn't do a thing for him, so he went back to Larry Parnes and told him so

but he also told him to keep Billy Fury away from him or he would drag him down with him,

In December, Larry Parnes Dropped Dickie, from the 1961 Big Beat Show Tour Spectaculars for mucking around too much,

The show would start with each star singing a line from a song, at rehearsals Cliff would start with

'One For the Money' and the spot would go on him, Billy Fury would then sing

'Two For the Show' and the spot would go on him, but when the spot would go on to where Dickie was,

he'd be lying on his back with sunglasses on, pretending to be sunbathing,

Parnes would get very annoyed and shout at everyone,

'Start again'

this time everyone would do their bit and when it got to Dickie he wouldn't be there,

instead, there'd be a voice coming out of the dark saying where is this spotlight supposed to be? I can't see in the dark.

Dickie used to be very rude to Parnes and threatened him in public,

but this made him very popular because Larry Parnes was so unpopular.

It was said that in the popularity stakes, if it was between Larry Parnes and Adolf Hitler, and they

88

stood next to each other, Larry Parnes would be more unpopular,

Dickie hated Parnes and Parnes Hated Dickie,

a lot of the reason being Dickie's attitude and his attraction to bad publicity and Parnes' opinion was that any bad publicity reflected on the others,

and several of them were heading for the Royal Variety Performances and into acting roles,

Parnes should have been more sympathetic,

but he had had a bad experience with Terry Dene who attracted very bad publicity early on in his career,

and the resulting storm was a very bad situation for all involved.

Terry Dene had appeared in court for drunkenness and vandalism and had been melodramatically discharged from the army during his national service after having a nervous breakdown.

shunned and discredited he was any manager's nightmare.

Parnes also thought that Dickie was totally underestimating his own talent, but it has to be said so was Larry Parnes.

Dickie was sabotaging his own career

and in the process could be sabotaging those people around him.

Larry Parnes was asked about Dickie Pride after Dickie's death, and he said surprisingly

"Dickie, poor Dickie, he died very young but there was an artiste. He made a wonderful album called *'Pride without Prejudice'* which I named. He had a superb recording voice and stage act; I remember Tommy Steele standing in the wings and saying' boy that fellow has got talent'.

Parnes wasn't about to risk any of his artists for the one, and when Dickie, probably hyped up on drugs, got into more trouble, Larry Parnes got rid of him,

The incident that was Dickie's downfall was an incident that Dickie somehow broke the arm of a woman stage assistant during a row.

It was all hushed up, but his probation officer was called and it was agreed that no further action would be taken,

But it was this that led him to lose his contract with Parnes, as he was still on probation,

Parnes had still not forgiven him for wrecking a dressing room and destroying a room in digs, a few months before.

After all it costs money to repair these things,

Dickie was boisterous and got into trouble, but he was still only a teenage boy.

By December because of Dickie's increasing erratic behaviour Parnes Dropped Him.

But thankfully Billy Fury his protector managed to persuade Parnes to take him back.

Billy Fury was Dickie's closest friend and an admirer of his.

Billy Fury and Dickie became the best of friends with Billy taking on the role of protector to Dickie Pride.

Dickie was loud, sometimes shy, but on other occasions, wild,

Always humorous, aggressive and was frequently under the influence in one form or another.

Whereas Billy was shy, warm, quiet, very gentle with a respect for everyone; they were the ying and yang, two different sides of the same coin and saw in each other qualities and personalities that they wish they had more of themselves.

Billy and Dickie lived together in Dickie's mum's house, with Dickie's mum and sister,

and as it was a small house Dickie and Billy used to share a double bed,

but obviously not as anything other than friends

The room was so small there was only the room for the double bed.

Dickie and Billy were blood brothers, they actually went as far as cutting their hands and rubbing them together, mingling the blood.

When Billy was to eventually leave Mrs. Kneller's house he was very upset because Mrs. Kneller was such a great cook,

he didn't want to leave.

Billy Fury, Joe Brown, Adam Faith and Marty Wilde used to meet up with the Vernon's girls at Dickie's house at Number 43 Heathfield Vale,

in South Croydon, where a bus would pick them all up.

The bus was usually driven by a man called Johnny Sparkes who liked to get to the next town pretty quickly so that he could find bookies, so that he could put a bet on.

these tours could be pretty boring bus journeys as you can imagine traveling from one place to another on the coach between gigs,

Dickie was so bored he would pass the time 'gurning' or pulling strange faces, Duffy would say to him,

Dickie pull this face, and he would, Dickie could never stay still and was full of life and would sit on the edge of a seat as if he was about to get up and do something,

 He was always up and about and always seeking attention like a small boy,

 Which in effect that's what he was

Other times he often seemed to be in a sulk,

looking back on it know he was probably suffering from depression even then, but in those days, it wasn't seen as normal to say you were depressed,

While traveling around on the bus he used to try and get some of the guys together and teach them how to sing in harmony, like a barbershop quartet, totally Cappello.

Georgie fame said, on the bus on the Timpson coach

on the Parnes tours Dickie was always trying to get us to sing four freshmen harmonies which for young rock 'n' roll kids like me,

was really radical stuff and he was going up and down

"You sing that, I'll sing that, you sing that,

and the four freshmen as you know were a fantastic close harmony singing group,

for young rock 'n' rollers like us that was really radical

and he was determined to get us to do it'.

Staying in digs was a nightmare some were good some were bad,

the dressing rooms in some of the theatres were the same, some were good some were bad,

with the good ones being locked and only opened for the real stars of the day such as Arthur Askey Morecombe and Wise etc.,

there was not a lot to do between getting to the venue and going on stage.

Larry Parnes caused a few problems between his boys as well, when Dickie released *'Primrose*

Lane' as a single Parnes also got Vince Eager to record the same song,

they were both released at the same time, no – one could understand the logic of this,

 because in effect the two records created a stalemate and cancelled each other's sales out, stopping either of them getting high in the charts, it should have been one artist or the other.

Dickies was the only version of the two to get into the charts and Dickie only got to number 28 in the charts for only one week.,

 but it was an entry, which he had not had before.

Dickie's problems usually started when he wasn't on stage,

he was unable to assert himself, he had no confidence,

he would do things indirectly, very different to the confident performer on stage,

 Duffy Power said "he used to ask for things in a wimpish way he wouldn't come up to you and say

'Hey Duffy, I liked that song of yours can I do it?',

instead, he would come up and say something about it being a good song, and how well I did it, and mumble all around it,

but would never get around to asking if he could perform it.

Dickie also had a cruel streak that would come out when he was bored,

he once sat on a lesbian's girls' knee on the tour bus and with a vicious spiteful look on his face he began kissing her,

and pulling her about until she was in tears,

no-one came to her rescue though.

If Johnny Gentle had been around Dickie wouldn't have gotten away with it.

Dickie has an argument with Terry Dene for missing his cue and being unprofessional and knocked him out backstage,

the result of this Dickie was distressed and smashed up a couple of dressing rooms,

Terry Dene

"I missed my cue for going on at the Liverpool Empire and Dickie Pride had to go on before me. He was really uptight about it and as soon as he came off stage, he smacked me right in the mouth

and he was swearing and hollering, and goodness knows what.

Finally, he went back to his dressing room and Billy Fury talked to me.

Billy was very laidback and very quiet, but he came out and said to me,

"Will you come and see Dickie because he's in a terrible state?'

Dickie was in there, crying his eyes out, and he was so apologetic for hitting me in the face and it was a funny thing because he was a nice guy.

I don't blame him for being angry. I should have been ready when my cue came up".

This resulted in Dickie's Probation officer being called in for a meeting with Larry Parnes

the result was that Dickie was dropped by Parnes again.

This time Billy Fury was unable to persuade Parnes to take Dickie back, for the moment.

This impossible situation took its toll on Dickie Pride who felt that he was trapped as Dickie Pride and he wanted to be Richard Kneller, who wanted to step out of the Dickie Pride Shadows and sing the kind of songs he wanted to sing the songs that he had sung on the excellent Pride without Prejudice Album.

Dorothy Orr:

Dickie Pride was shy but completely potty on stage, he drove everywhere in his two-seater red sports car during shows and after he would take Gene Vincent for a quick spin, Gene liked and respected Dickie very much,

Marty Wilde and Billy Fury were often at Dickie's house, Billy Fury lived there for a while, Billy Fury had a red car which was the bane of the neighbours life he overturned it once, Joe Brown, Adam Faith, Marty Wilde and the Vernon's girls used to congregate at Dickie's house and a coach would come to pick them all up, Dickie used to drive a red Austin Healey Sprite.

Dickie used to call Marty Wilde dad who he was close friends with, Marty used to call him son, nothing to do with their age but a reflection on their comparative heights

Dickie signed with the Noel Grey agency, and appeared on a television program called Riverboat shuffle where he sang

'Bye Bye Blackbird', but it was another failed television pop show,

he did the rounds doing interviews and photo sessions for girl's magazines including Meet the beat magazine

who did a successful line of booklets called meet …Billy Fury, Marty Wilde, the Beatles etc. the booklet Meet... Dickie Pride was never released.

But there was not a lot of work about, so he spent most of his time writing music.

Dickie did make attempts at writing his own music, but it looks like none of his music has survived while Dickie was experimenting with Jazz and Latin music which he found was uncommercial even though his efforts were brilliant his fondness for drugs and drink meant that it was impossible to concentrate on writing new music he was usually under the influence of something making him loud aggressive wild and also humorous

On October the 20th he was brought back in front of the courts for breaching his probation,

For' failing to lead an industrious life'.

He explained that he was writing music.

Dickie stood in the dock at the Croydon Magistrates court again and was told by the magistrate Mr. H Needham.

'Everyone in this country has got to keep himself and he doesn't eat if he doesn't earn the money.

there is plenty of other work and it is up to you to find a job that will bring you a weekly wage, even if it is not in the theatrical line'.

Dickie who was nineteen at the time and was in front of the court for breach of his probation order which was imposed at the West Kent Sessions in 1959 for attempted shop breaking and driving away a motor scooter (which he had done as a joke) without consent,

. his probation officer Mr. P A Seal said,

'He had failed to lead an industrious life and had not reported regularly, he lives at home with his mother, and I'm sorry to say that she has to go out to work to keep him'.

By this time if you got one gig a week it was worth a week's wages to a normal job,

It was well paid, but you had to work hard to find that gig a week.

His career since then was described by Mr. Seal, as

'In December 1960 he had a disagreement with his agent and his contract was terminated', he said

'Since then, he has not worked regularly and has been attached to some agency in London, his contracts have been far and few between'.

And he had trouble facing life in reality,

Dickie said to the court that he had no income for the last five weeks.

'But I might have sold 25,000 records, I don't know, I get paid royalties quarterly.

He said about working,

'If I'm writing a piece of music then I'm working.

Some people compose music and get nothing for twenty years.

The question of course is what has happened to this music? does it exist? if so, has it survived?

what is known is that Dickie could write music, and could read it,

as he once demonstrated when he wrote a song for Billy Fury that took the Mickey out of Larry

Parnes, and about how gay he was this was called 'The Parnes Anthem'.

Or did he have a problem writing at that time because of his addiction to drugs,

as the first thing to go is usually the power of concentration, who knows?

but it would be very interesting to hear it if it ever turns up.

Dickies probation order was extended, and he was advised to take what work he could.

Duffy Power:

 Dickie had the ability to do anything, he could have walked it, there was tons of work out there and the Beatles only increased it, but Dickie never did get out and try to get work, he just didn't know how'.

1962

Another tour
Corum Mansions
Getting Married

Billy Fury managed to get Dickie booked on a Parnes tour, this was a major tour called

'Big Star-Spangled night'

With Marty Wilde, Karl Denver, Peter Jay and the Jaywalkers, Eden Kane and of course Billy Fury.

Traveling to far out places, such as Great Yarmouth, on the Essoldo circuit

It was during this tour that Dickie returned home and got into an argument with his mother and blacked her eye and according to Hal Carter,

he broke her finger, the police were called, but no action was taken against Dickie, it was also at this time that he split once again with his girlfriend Mandy whom he had been going out with on and off since his schooldays.

This was the final time

and they both went their separate ways.

Mandy Said: I wasn't still in love with him, but there was a tremendous affection and loyalty, I didn't want to feel that I was dumping him, there was a thread that could have only been broken by death, Dickie started taking drugs when he met Lionel Bart and his friends, he was easily led, he used to tell me about drugs, he was a gentle man, fun loving, always laughing and with a ready smile, he had a sympathetic and enquiring mind, he was an intelligent man but eventually he became someone that I didn't know'.

Within six months of this split both he and Mandy were married to other people.

On March the 21st Dickie gets married to Patricia Anne Arkell at Holborn registry office, they were both aged twenty years of age,

 his profession was described as Entertainer, hers is described as a Model she was an American, and may have been a Tiller girl, she took her pet Chihuahua Polo with her,

Both Dickie and she were living together at no 4 Coram Mansions, Millman Street W1

Patricia was known as Tricia and she was a cigarette girl at the Astor club, it was suspected that she may have done some whoring to supplement her income,

 although this is only speculation, but it's likely that most of the girls did this at one time or another.

Tricia was known to be hard, but her flat was tidy and there was nothing tacky about Tricia. Both Dickie and her were into dope and she would sell her cigarettes down at the Astor, come back with the money and they would spend it on dope, Dickie wanted to roll the perfect joint, Duffy went away and came back four years later, and he was still trying to roll the perfect joint.

Tricia had a flat in Corum mansions Corum street, Holborn in 1961, Dickie moved in with her, on the day that they moved in together I was at a gig that day, I remember I bought a dozen eggs for them and they were thrilled, I parked myself on Dickie and Tricia and I was welcome there but I moved out one day when they had one of their rows, there was a terrible row I could hear in the bedroom one night and afterwards they sort of went to bed the light stayed on all night with music going it was that type of scene and I just up and left them, I looked them up a couple of years later they were living in Bayswater when I got there they were still doing the same thing in the same position still trying to roll the perfect joint, there was trouble between Dickie and Tricia, the neighbours described Dickie screaming as if his wife was beating him she was only a small woman but certainly she did have the ability.

According to Duffy

"She was a hardnosed girl, but was very ladylike and there was nothing tacky about her'

Her mentor was Lee Everett (Disc jockey Kenny Everett's wife)

who was Queen Bea of the girls at the time, and they all hung around her,

Now that they were married Dickie had moved in with Tricia,

on the day that Dickie had moved in with Tricia, Duffy Power visited them

Duffy is supposed to have had a flat with Dickie, but this isn't the case,

Duffy and Dickie did live together but this was also with Tricia,

One day Duffy left his mum's house and parked himself on Dickie and Tricia's sofa and was made very welcome.

Duffy eventually moved out one day after Dickie and Tricia had had an argument, Duffy said

"They had one of their rows, they started rowing, there was a terrific noise that I could hear from the bedroom and after that they sort of went to bed,

the light stayed on all night long,

Dimmed with music going on,

Duffy moved back in with the two of them again, but left again when the trouble between them started again,

With Dickie, being beaten by his wife.

By this time, they had a son Richard (Ricky) junior.

It was rumoured that he wasn't in fact Dickies son the boy's father was Joe Moretti the lead guitarist with Johnny Kidd and the pirates who played the iconic riff from their hit shaking all over, it's a fact that he was very close to Tricia at one time but looking at the photographs of Richard over the years it's quiet obvious that he is Dickies son.

Dickies wife Tricia Ludt said when I interviewed her in 2001 that:

I don't really want to talk about Dickie, but I will say this:

'Richard was devious, violent and a bit of a shit, but he could be loveable and funny, I loved him at one time, and we shared a lot of good times together for a while, we even had a son together, but he got too dependent on the drugs, so we parted ways.

I was devastated when he died, but it didn't really come as too much of a surprise, I came over to England for the funeral and I met up with Richard's sister Ann'.

Duffy Said

' Dickie was an education on stage, his act was quiet dynamic, and he was about the only one the other singers would go to the side of the stage to watch,

 and even though Dickie was low on the bill he would close the first half which is like third on the bill,

 he would run up to the drums and play the drums and he would run up to the piano and play the piano,

 It was pretty dramatic, other singers didn't do that because they couldn't play anything',

'Dickie hated pop music he liked rock but not pop he called it "Ricky-Tic" music he'd make a face and move his hand up with the rhythm and say it's Ricky tic',

it can be pretty difficult when you are two people remembering who you are, in the end I think he was more concerned with what was happening to Richard Kneller rather than Dickie Pride

– it wasn't Dickie Pride that was going to end up working in the sausage factory'.

Dickie did a gig at the Dancehall in South End Dickie was backed by the paramount's who were

Bob Scott vocals

Garry booker keyboards

Robin Trower guitar

Chris Copping bass

Mick Braintree drums

On April 12th he appeared on the BBC light program which was presented by Saturday Club at the Royal Albert Hall it featured The Oscar

Robin band, Adam Faith, The Lana Sisters, Craig Douglas, Duffy Power, Dickie Pride, The John Barry 7, and Bert Weedon and the Trebbletones, the compere was Brian Mathews

On April 20th he started another tour for Parnes Billy Fury had talked Parnes round again.

Starting At Portsmouth Guildhall Called an Evening with Billy Fury.

April 22nd	Croydon ABC
April 23rd	Derby Gaumont
April 24th	St Albans Gaumont
April 25th	Bournemouth Gaumont
May 4th	Worcester Gaumont
May 5th	Birmingham Hippodrome

The Promoter Was Larry Parnes

Featuring Billy Fury, the Tornadoes, Mike Preston, Mike and Tony Nevitt, the Echoes, Dickie Pride, Compere Larry Burns

Dickie did another summer season for Parnes over summer at the Great Yarmouth Britannia Theatre, the dates were July 7th, July 14th, July

21st July 23rd July 28th, July 30th, August 4th, August 11th, August 18th, August 25th, Sept 1st, Sept 8th, Sept 15th, this was called the Sunday special featuring, Billy Fury, The Tornadoes, Freddy and The Dreamers, Tommy Bruce, Mike Preston Mike and Tony Nevitt And The Barron Knights the Compere Was Al Page.

Also, the Rest of the Dates Were July 28th, August 4th, Aug 11th Aug 18th Aug 25th

These Shows featured Joe Brown and his bruvvers Freddie and the Dreamers

On the 11th and 21st August, the acts were, Maureen Evans Mike Preston, Vince Eager Mike and Tony Nesbitt the Barron Knights with Duke Diamond Dickie Pride and the Compere was Al Page

On 20th of October Dickie again went to court in answer to the earlier court appearance of September 1960,

and didn't he get scrutinized by the courts,

his whole career up to that time was analysed,

it was pointed out that on one side was the boy who could earn £30 in twenty minutes as a pop star and on the other side there was the serious student of music who had trained at Canterbury Cathedral and who hated the pop star side of him,

it was also pointed out that in his opinion if he had been allowed to continue his studies after his father had died, he would not have become a pop star.

Dickie said that in the three years that he had been in show business he had not had a break, but could not work now and had a lot of difficulties,

his probation officer Mr. Seal said

"His behaviour on probation has been erratic and he apparently found it difficult to face reality". The chairman Mr. Tristan Beresford Q C, directed that the order should continue and be extended to three years he told Dickie

"Don't go on being temperamental but take your engagements, will you do that?" Dickie agreed to do so.

Outside the court Dickie threw his arms around his mum saying

"Silly old mum, I told you it would be alright" she was convinced that Dickie was going to jail.

1963

The Beatles

The Guv'nors

Car crash

1963 Started out as a good year for Dickie he began to put the past behind him at last.

Billy Fury once again comes to Dickie's rescue and gets him booked on another Parnes tour , Dickie had met Billy Fury in November 1958 and the two become firm friends from the beginning, Billy became Dickies closest friend and protector from Larry Parnes, stopping Parnes from sacking Dickie on a few occasions he was a sort of fairy godfather to Dickie, the show was called the 'Thank Your Lucky Stars' Tour, at short notice, Billy was already suffering from the effects of the heart disease that was eventually going to take his life,

he needed Dickie to fill in for him on nights that he couldn't go on,

Duffy Power, fellow musician, and flat mate and great friend to Dickie Pride and Billy Fury:

'Billy was a shy, warm, gentle and a quiet man in many ways Billy and Dickie were the Yin and Yang, two very different sides of the same coin, both seeing in each other parts of a personality they wish they had more of'.

Dickie and Billy both had great talent musically if they had both survived to today who knows what they could have both achieved as solo artists in their own rights or as a fantastic collaboration of both of them who would have given Lennon and Mc Cartney a run for their money, despite Billy Fury's efforts to save Dickie from himself he was unable to do so and Dickie went to an early grave'.

Dickie was backed by the echoes.

But became very fed up with working more and more second-rate dance halls. and with unknown bands.

As he became lesser known his wages dropped and so did the quality of the backing bands.

After all you had to have a record in the charts to pull in the crowds.

Dickie loved being on tour and he was never happier than when he was on stage singing for an appreciative audience, he was now beginning to get on top of his troubles.

At this time there was so much work for him that he signed with the George Cooper Organization who ran a very dire group of dance halls called the Ron King dance halls,

which had a reputation for Teddy boy trouble, but they were never that much trouble to Dickie, a natural funny guy.

he would come out with some great one liner, and he generally won them over with stunts on stage,

such as brief spells on the drums,

then running over to the piano and playing a tune on that,

playing the saxophone and his incredible shake routine,

a sprinkling of comedy and he sang some great numbers, usually from the Ray Charles repertoire,

and arrangements that he had picked up while he was working with Gene Vincent and Eddie Cochran back in 1960,

Songs such as

'what'd I Say' or 'Sticks and Stones' or as a last resort Jumping off stage and punching the offender

Dickie was well known for giving the odd head butt,

Duffy Power was also there on the bill working as a separate act,

Dickie's marriage by this time was beyond repair so he and Duffy took a flat together in Bayswater but after that, things go quiet,

Until in April George Cooper decided to get three of his acts together,

to form a trio a super group.

so, with Nelson Keane (an ex Parnes protégé) and Bobby Shafto they form a group called 'the Guv'nors' and in April they release a record called 'Let's Make a Habit of It 'on the Piccadilly label number 7n 35117

The B side was called 'The Kissing had to stop',

Dickie was working hard, and his life was going well, and it looked as this group may do well judging by the new record which was very good,

Dickie tried to make a comeback he was booked onto the 'Thank Your Lucky Stars' Television show, ITV'S major pop show,

 others appearing on the show were the Beatles Who were the headliners, it was advertised in the NME with a photograph of Dickie with the Beatles who recorded 'Please Please Me,'. this was the start of the Beatles' reign.

 Dickie's career suffered a major setback. The Single did not do well.

 But Dickie is in top form.

 But disaster struck again when Bobbie Shafto who was making a personal appearance was seriously injured in a car crash in Germany,

 he and a colleague Fred Clifford who was Dickie's financial advisor at the time were involved in a road crash outside Ingolstadt on the Nuremburg to Munich autobahn,

 Bobby Shafto was seriously injured but Fred Clifford was killed,

 This finished 'The Guv'nors',

1963 was the last year of big bookings for Dickie but he still worked.

When the Beatles and Mersey beat era came along a lot of the solo acts were swamped, no one was spared, and teenagers wanted everything to be sung by Merseyside groups the solo artist was out by 1963.

There were a few exceptions Tommy Steele became a Hollywood star who appealed to everyone, especially parents.

Billy Fury had limited success probably because he was from Liverpool as well and was able to go with the flow for a while,

but his ill health destroyed his career eventually.

Georgie Fame did well but he was destined to do so from the beginning anyway, Going by his performances, as a member of the Larry Parnes stable.,

 Ironically, he turned to Jazz and become one of the major stars of the era in exactly the field of music that Dickie was now interested in,

Marty Wilde and Duffy Power did a couple of R and B singles, each did well.

Duffy jumped tracks and turned to Jazz, fading away for a few years,

 he had his own problems,

 but later in the 60's he became something big in the blues field.

The Sad and ironic thing was that the youngsters wanted exactly the same music that was being recorded in the late 50's early 60's By Billy, Marty, and all the other Parnes artists

but they had to be rerecorded by bands

the songs were mainly from the Ray Charles, Chuck Berry back catalogue,

But obviously these tunes were all new to them and the fifties was a different decade.

Dickie turned to Rhythm and Blues.

Dickie again worked for the Larry Parnes organization

deputizing for Billy Fury who was becoming more ill as time went on,

Being backed by the Echoes,

with Billy's fading health and not being able to perform, the venues, started to become more and more second rate as did the musicians who backed him.

In October Dickie Started another Tour starting on the 4th at   Croydon ABC,

Oct 5th   Brighton Essoldo

Oct 6th   Plymouth ABC

Oct 7th   Exeter ABC

Oct 8th	Southampton ABC
Oct 9th	Hastings ABC
Oct 10th	Dover ABC
Oct 11th	Bexley Heath ABC
Oct 12th	Ipswich Gaumont
Oct 13th	Cambridge Regal
Oct 14th	Northampton ABC
Oct 15th	Chesterfield ABC
Oct 16th	Lincoln ABC
Oct 17th	Cleethorpes ABC
Oct 18th	Hull ABC
Oct 19th	Scarborough Futurist
Oct 20th	Stockton Globe
Oct 26th	Doncaster Gaumont
Oct 27th	Carlisle ABC
Oct 28th	Huddersfield ABC
Oct 29th	Ardwick ABC
Oct 30th	Gloucester ABC
Oct 31st	Romford ABC
Nov 1st	Kingston ABC
Nov 2nd	Walthamstow Granada

Nov 3rd	Coventry Theatre
Nov 4t	Walthamstow Rank
Nov 5th	Walthamstow Rank
Nov 6th	Southend Rank
Nov 7th	Tooting Granada
Nov 8th	Cardiff Rank
Nov 9th	Bournemouth Winter Gardens
Nov 10th	Leicester De Montfort Hall
Nov 15th	Shrewsbury Granada
Nov 16th	Blackpool Opera House
Nov 17th	Liverpool Empire
Nov 18th	Bradford Gaumont
Nov 19th	Sunderland Rank
Nov 20th	York Rialto
Nov 21st	Sheffield Odeon
Nov 22nd	Derby Rank
Nov 23rd	Henley Rank
Nov 24th	Birmingham Hippodrome
Nov 25th	Worcester Rank
Nov 26th	Cheltenham Rank
Nov 27th	Taunton Rank

Nov 28th	St Albans Rank
Nov 29th	Guildford Rank
Nov 30th	Portsmouth Guild Hall
Dec 1st	Bristol Colston Hall
Dec 7th	Norwich Theatre Royal
Dec 8th	Rochester Odeon
Dec 9th	Colchester Odeon
Dec 10th	Harrow Granada
Dec 11th	Bedford Granada
Dec 12th	Mansfield Granada
Dec 13th	Sutton Granada
Dec 14th	Slough Adelphi
Dec 15th	Woolwich Granada
Dec 16th	Edmonton Granada

Featuring Billy Fury, Joe Brown, Dickie Pride, Karl Denver Trio, The Tornadoes Marty Wilde, Daryl Quist The Ramblers, Freddy and the dreamers, Compere Larry Burns,

Promoted by Larry Parnes.

On November the 4th Dickie and Billy Fury were involved in a major car accident on the M1, Dickie was unhurt but Billy Fury was taken to hospital with Concussion and a broken arm,

they were lucky, it could have been another Eddie Cochran and Johnny Kidd scenario where there was yet another Rock and roll Road fatality.

On Wednesday the 6th of November they had recovered enough to appear at the Odeon in Southend for a Parnes show

alongside Joe Brown, Karl Denver, the Tornados, Marty Wilde, Daryl Quist, Larry Burns and the Ramblers.

On November the 18th Dickie Appeared on another Parnes tour at the Gaumont ballroom, Bradford

with Billy Fury, Joe Brown, the Karl Denver trio, the Tornadoes, Marty Wilde, Daryl Quist, Larry Burns and The Ramblers.

1964

Polydor
Bluebeat
Black Bobby

Polydor records wanted Dickie to sign for them and to put him under contract as a Rock and Roll singer,

he even went as far as going to Polydor records offices for a chat

but he backed out when he found out that they only wanted him to record rock and roll,

which Dickie didn't want to do, as he felt he had outgrown his old rock and roll ways, so he refused to sign, so no contract.

Dickie was always a reluctant rock and roller,

he was more interested in singing and was now into Jazz and Blues orientated songs,

this may be because of his classical upbringing, this seemed to be a logical progression.

A strange phenomenon developed in 1964 called Bluebeat, it was very popular with the mods

which was a strange mix of Blues music, a mix of calypso and a bit of Beat music mixed in, it came from Jamaica and was the music that was specially created for people to dance to, it can be described as the forerunner to today's Reggae music,

it developed fast in this country due to the increase of West Indian immigration communities.

the main act in the blue beat boom was a star called Prince Buster,

the national weekly music papers even had their own blue beat charts,

but it was another performer who managed to get blue beat into the mainstream charts,

his name was Ezz Reco, and a sixteen-year-old Jamaican girl called Millie Small

(who in a couple of years would have a number two hit in the national charts called 'My Boy Lollipop')

with a song called 'King of Kings' his group was called Ezz Reco's Launchers' under the banner of Island records.

The major record companies, never slow at picking up on the latest musical craze realized that this music was appealing to not only young black kids and they jumped on the bandwagon and started to push their inferior products

 but also, to young white kids (mods), so they started to release Blue Beat records of their own, these were inferior records made with the same type of style as the originals but nowhere near as good,

 but hyped up to the hilt with such acts as 'the Beavers' and 'Jimmy Nichol and The Shudups'

 Who were Cyril Stapleton's Orchestra (Beavers) and Dickie Pride (Jimmy Nichol and the Shudups),

 Who was working with Cyril Stapleton at the time

It's while working with the Cyril Stapleton Band That Dickie Was said to have tried Heroin for the first time.

Dickie's self-esteem was hitting an all-time low,

At this time Dickie was hanging around with various jazz musicians' people like Zoot Money, Long John Baldry, Julie Driscoll, Rod Stewart and Brian Auger, this was not to say that this lot were involved in the drug scene, and he was getting deeper and deeper into the drugs scene.

Dickie got involved with a couple called Georgina Shaw and Gavin Shaw they were brother and sister, who had a flat Off Regent Street, Park Road she became the manager of the Sidewinders

it was a slum, they used to run a band called 'The Sidewinders',

'The Sidewinders were a blues orientated band similar to 'The Blue Flames', but a bit more bluesy,

they gigged up and down the country.

Duffy Power was offered the gig, but he refused,

They were formed and built around Dickie's singing style to accompany Dickie's swinging vocal style.

as he was seen as one of the best in the business at this time.

as well as accompanying Dickie they performed instrumentals ranging from swing to doo wop the band were

On Guitar Len Nelbett

On Cornet Marc Charig

On Piano Mathew Hutchinson

On Bass Tex Makins

On Sax Johnny Marshal

On Drums Malcolm Penn

On Congas Jimmy Scott

They were managed by Georgina Shaw.

Boz Burrell joined them later to fill in when Dickie Became absent and usually covering Dickie when he was laid out because of drugs, he coped so well that on Dickie's return he was kept on as a second vocalist.

One of the gigs that the Sidewinders did regularly was at a venue called

'The Roaring 20's a quite well-known club in London,

Before the club opened one evening Dickie was in the corridor of the club and Duffy Power was there and there was an altercation with one of the staff and a young guy in some type of uniform.

He was looking at Dickie sort of eyeing him up and mumbled something to Dickie,

Dickie did not like what he had said to him,

he was eyeing this guy up as if he was going to hit him and Dickie was heard clearly muttering to himself

'No not again, no don't do it, no not again no not this time no no no' and the guy looked at him and backed off and walked away.

Dickie said'

thank God I didn't hit him and that I didn't do it' Duffy just looked at Dickie, puzzled at the time Dickie was well known for his flying head butt, where he would run at a crowd of people, fans usually, head butt someone and then pull them down on top [of him, and use that guy as a shield against the others as they were trying to kick him.

Duffy Power:

A lot of Showbiz people used to meet at the Shaw's flat because they were known in drug circles,

 they used to sit around and listen to jazz records and musicians, Dickie met up with a girl called Black Bobbie, there weren't many black girls around in those days, she was quite famous at the time

 so, Dickie was fascinated, so they paired off, Black Bobbie was also fascinated with white people and she lived there with Dickie for a while, she was a heroin addict, she helped to get Dickie further into harder drugs, she wasn't into Heroin when I first met her, she then became a Heroin addict, I think it was convenient for her to stay at Park road and she stayed in a room with Dickie, as far as I know it was from her that Dickie developed his Heroin addiction, if it was an addiction as it's not guaranteed to be an addiction, but he started taking heroin'.

there were quite a few names who used to congregate at Park Road, mainly jazz musicians and one or two R and B singers including Duffy Powers, Mike Prater, Elton Dean, Marc Charig and sometimes John Coltraine and Rod Stewart this is not a suggestion that they were into drugs though.

On July 12th Dickie Performed at Leeds Queens Hall, on the bill were the Rolling Stones, Lulu and the Lovers Ray Anton and the Peppermint Men Myles Brother with Dallas, Ray Herron and the Guvnors

But work soon dried up and Dickie was out of work and unable to get a singing job.

By Late 1964 Dickie was so desperate for work that he took a job as a store man at the Singer Sewing machine factory in South London.

Dickie had stopped drinking at this time and was just starting his journey into hard drugs.

Then Things started to look up and he got some work singing again.

He got a job working on the Ron King Dancehalls with a band called The Puppets (who went on to back Gene Vincent on a British Tour)

Dickie was fantastic,

where Songs such as Sticks and Stones were showstoppers.

The Ron King Dancehalls were tough but so was Dickie often jumping down off the stage to knock someone out then returning to stage without dropping a beat saying

" I'm Getting paid for making a fool of myself what's your excuse"

But working for Ron King Didn't work out for Dickie and he quickly moved on to the next agency.

1965

Ricky

Joe Meek

Duffy Power

In 1965 Dickie signs with the John Gunnel agency.) with The Original Topics who were Nicky Graham, John Horton, and Roger Groom who played the drums.

While Dickie was singing with a jazz orientated rhythm and blues group in the evening.

They appeared on George Mellys Jazz beat show on BBC radio where they recorder four numbers, Walking, little boy don't get scared, sack o woe and moody mood my love

It was at this time that he got himself a new manager Alan Wheeler and for the next six months he tried everything that he could to get people interested in Dickie Pride and his career, Dickie was singing with the Original Topics on a semi pro basis he worked for the Singer Sewing Machine Company during the day; he had to have some money coming in regularly as he had a baby on the way,

Alan Wheeler:

I first met Dickie in 1959 backstage at the Romford Odeon where I worked as a projectionist for stage shows, I changed over to stagehand/ follow spot operator, I had to assist the artists like Gene Vincent, Marty Wilde, Cliff Richard etc with mike stands or work up in the box but I also came into regular contact with Larry Parnes. He offered me a job with LMP Enterprises as office boy cum secretary of the Marty Wilde fan club, where I again came into contact with Dickie Pride while on the tour bus at times for the Rock n Trad Spectacular package tours.

In 1961 when we had both departed Parnes' set up, When I took up managing Dickie in 1965 he was into Jazz orientated Rhythm and Blues, which wasn't the most commercial field to be in at the time, he was doing his best to shake off the Shiek of Shake image which did him no favours as Dickie would simply refuse to do Rock n Roll bookings, Joe Meek invited Dickie to audition for him at his Holloway road studio (if you can call them that)

Dickie, myself and the guitarist from the original topics (Nicky Graham? Maybe) went along one evening, Meek was a quietly spoken man of few words quickly getting down to the nitty gritty of putting something on tape, it was a complete shambles, how on earth ordinary discs let alone hits, were produced there is beyond belief, but it shows how clever he was and definitely ahead of his time, I did not like the man although he wanted to record Dickies version of 'out of sight' he recorded it with just a guitar backing, Meek was happy with the result and he promised to find Dickie a song to record,

The trouble with Joe Meek as I later learned that he rapidly loses interest in a project if things don't come together quickly and that is what happened, he never found the song for Dickie and the project fizzled out, a great pity as Dickie needed a disc to get him back into the limelight,

Polydor expressed an interest in recording Dickie, and they invited him up to their offices for a chat, this was in 1965, but Dickie withdrew when he discovered that they were only interested in recording him as the Sheik of

Shake, he didn't want and wouldn't turn the clock back to Rock n Roll.

In the end we parted company due to conflict of musical direction, a few bookings were coming in for Rock n Roll gigs, but Dickie wasn't having any of it and I couldn't break him into the field he wanted to pursue due to his past reputation

I did manage to set up a gig for Dickie and the band The group played at a pop festival that was being built around 'Heinz'

which was at the Co-op Hall, in Hallstead in Essex, on the understanding that Dickie would play more commercial music and drop the jazz orientated music,

he went on and performed 'Out of Sight' which was very well received, he usually started with 'Diana' by Paul Anka.

and then went into a bunch of Mose Allison and Jelly Roll Morton Compositions, which were totally lost on that type of audience, who had just been listening to

'Just like Eddie' by Heinz,

it was a great act, but to the wrong audience.

The group decided to cut an Ep demo disc at the Morden recording studios, four songs were recorded one was James Brown' 'Out of Sight' and another one was 'Get on The Right Track Baby' which was later recorded by Georgie Fame and the Blue Flames.

The Ep was submitted to Mike Hawker A and R man for Fontana, who also wrote songs for Dusty Springfield, Helen Shapiro and others,

He used to work for Parnes, it was submitted under the name of Dickie Pride and the Original Topics,

who were Nicky Graham, Johnny Horton and Roger Groom But they were turned down.

it may have been that he knew Dickie from the early days as he worked for Larry Parnes, and he knew Dickie's reputation and abilities and he knew how unpredictable Dickie could be.

One minute he could be hilariously funny, the next minute he could be rude and aggressive.

A bit like Gene Vincent was but Gene Vincent was more polite or courteous. Such was his temperament

He was enthusiastic about the record but decided that it wasn't for Fontana another setback it was not what Dickie wanted to hear,

this wasn't guaranteed to put you on Dickie's side so not to be disheartened they took the EP to a couple of smaller labels

The Ep was taken to Ember records and Starlight records who also turned them down.

Whatever happened to these recordings, who now owns them?

After this Dickies career virtually faded, and he never recovered from this constant run of bad luck, which seemed to be hounding him.

On April 10th the sound of Jimmy Nichol appeared on the Saturday club with Adam Faith, Freddie and The Dreamers, Martha and the Vandellas, the animals, the roulettes, the Silkie and Tommy Sanderson.

In 1965 the sound of Jimmy Nichol released a single on the Decca Label Number F12107 Called, A side, Clementine, B side, Bim Bam

On May the 11th Dickie's son Ricky was born at the Weir maternity hospital, Balham, South London the Address of both parents is given as Flat 1, 75 Christchurch Road, Tulse Hill, South London, although Dickie wasn't living there by this time, he has written his profession as 'Sewing Machine store man' on the birth certificate.

 it was rumoured at the time that Dickie's son was not Dickie's but was the child of session musician Joe Moretti's,

 the man who was made famous for his guitar lick on the Johnny Kidd and the Pirates hit 'Shakin' All Over'

 but photographs of Dickie's son shown over the years prove this statement to be wrong

the likeness to Dickie is too significant for him to be anyone else' son,

 This was confirmed when he appeared in London at the opening of the stage play about Dickie's / his father's life written by Charles Langley in 1999.

 He was the spitting image of his father.

The truth is that the marriage was dead in the water and Dickie was now spending most of his time at another of Parnes' former protégé's Duffy Power,

Dickie was slowly getting deeper and deeper into all kinds of drugs.

Duffy Said

Dickie said to him

"You'll be alright after all this" he said, he looked slightly mean just a tad resentful he said

"Your one of those people"

he could see such a thing that he had something in himself that wasn't controllable that he didn't know how to deal with, and it could in the end do him in'.

Dickie was into Amyl Nitrate which he used to inject, I would only skin pop and did it only about a dozen times, but Dickie was really into it and used to say skin Poppin wasn't proper, one day he took the needle and just rammed it into his knee through his trousers, I knew then he wasn't a proper addict it was something else.

Dickie told me once, and he wouldn't have told me this if it wasn't true, and it shows how crazy he could be, Theres a thing called Amyl Nitrate it came in a little glass tube with a little muslin bag all around it so that the glass doesn't fall all over the place it contained a vapour, very very powerful and he used to grab his mother, his little old Welsh mother, almost a stereotypical Welsh woman, getting on a bit, and he used to grab her and snap these Amyl Nitrate and put them under her nose and she used to curse him, she'd say oh Dickie, totally stoned out of her head'.

Dickie couldn't get a recording contract, and didn't know about how to get work or couldn't be bothered or was just too lazy or the drugs were affecting him,

although if he really wanted to work, he could have, he had the ability to do anything,

Because of the Beatles boom and the Mersey beat boom there was a lot of work about at the time

but he really didn't try or was too choosy or he just did not know how to go about it'.

Dickie nearly cracked it with Joe Meek,

the lead guitarist with his band 'The Original Topics' Nicky Graham, and Dickie recorded onto tape 'Out of Sight', and three other tracks

The recorded tracks which have never surfaced to this day and have not been heard and it's not known what the other tracks are.

which may be in the tea chest tapes,

a bunch of recorded tapes that were kept in tea chests and were only found after joe Meek had died,

Alan Blackburn is the only person to have listened to all the tapes and said that he can't remember hearing Dickie

but he may not have remembered his voice and Joe meek didn't write the correct things on the tape boxes to mislead people who were trying to steal the songs.

'Out Of Sight' was a number 24 hit for James Brown in 1964,

Meek was a quietly spoken man he is impressed by what he hears and promises to find Dickie or write Dickie a hit, if he could find the right material,

But it was only Rock And roll that Meek was interested in,

but Dickie insisted on recording the music that he was interested in so 'Out of sight' was committed to tape with just a guitar to back him there was just a quick run through with Meek running in to adjust the mike and then it was committed to tape

But Meek lost interest as things were not going to plan, so he changed his mind Sadly this wasn't to be,

and Dickie never recorded for the dynamite RGM sound of Joe Meek, at 304 Holloway Road,

He was furious with Joe Meek; Dickie never forgave him.

But it looked as if his reputation was working against him.

it would have been a great boost to Dickie's ego as well, which he could have done with at that time.

By this time Dickie has found a new musical interest in Jazz and South American rhythms, those that heard Dickie Pride all agree that Dickie was very good.

It was at this time that Dickie and Duffy took LSD, they had never had it before,

so, Dickie, Duffy and a friend of theirs who was a guitarist, went back to Duffy's place in Queenwood Gardens in Bayswater and took the stuff,

it was on a sugar cube, the guitarist decided that he wanted some cigarettes, so Duffy and Dickie went to get them for him it wasn't far from Hyde Park,

they were carried away with the trip which they were enjoying,

Duffy says that he regressed He was now an American Indian about to attack the fort

so, he picked up a stick and decided to charge a tree,

and they got a good rush out of it as they tore past on their horses,

so, they hurtled down a slope towards a tree and Duffy threw a stick, 'wham' it hit the tree, Dickie threw his stick but he lost his balance and he took a great tumble and hit the deck,

they went and lay under some trees at a point where two paths crossed, and Dickie lay down at this point and Duffy sees Dickie as a crucified Christ child

'I asked him what he was waiting for and he said

" I am waiting to be loved'. The love he needed had gone with his father.

before they went back to Duffy's flat they sat down on a seat in Paddington station,

Duffy said that he looked at Dickie really closely and saw in Dickie a beautiful child again,

all the hardness usually in his face was gone and there was no pain,

and he had beautiful eyes, Duffy Power was not gay, he explains that it was just the way that he saw Dickie at that time,

it was just the beauty of the moment and Duffy said to him

"I know why I like you" and he just nodded and said" I know you do" and that was that they had forgotten about the poor guitarist,

when they got back to the flat, he had left a note saying 'Thank you' in big sarcastic letters,

At another time while under the influence of one drug or another they went into a park because they believed they were knights in shining Armor.

They were approached by a dog, and they ran back to their flat and hid in terror because they thought that it was a fire breathing Dragon.

Alan Wheeler was Dickie's manager for a short time in 1965, Dickie was persuaded by Alan Wheeler to go along to the George Cooper Organization in Soho Square, who were signing up all the old faces including Vince Eager, Marty Wilde, Joe Brown and their newest signing was Johnny Kidd And The Pirates, Alan Wheelers usual band, and While Dickie was there Duffy Power was there for the same reason, the result was that Dickie and Duffy were signed as separate acts but were playing the same dates as the same theatres and were often backed by a band called 'The Puppets' who were Gene Vincent's band at a Blackpool season in 1965.

Dickie performed one or two Rhythm and Blues numbers 'What'd I Say 'and Sticks and Stones using the Ray Charles arrangements picked up from working with Eddie Cochran and Gene Vincent in 1960.

Dickie's wife had now left him taking his son Richard junior (Ricky) with her, she returned to America to live; he was in debt and owed quite a bit of Money, his phone had been cut off and he was a very hard man to contact, he could only be contacted by telegram, making it very very difficult to reach him in a hurry,

 Even, if he was easy to get hold of. His reluctance to conform and go along the Rock and Roll route or the commercial route would have still made it difficult to have given him a recording contract anyway.

Hal Carter, Larry Parnes' deputy Said:

"Dickie God rest his soul, was possibly the best vocalist and musician of the lot.

He certainly had the talent, built in talent but he destroyed it he was into bad habits, nobody told dickie what to do, and in fact if you told him something to do, he'd do the opposite, not that he wanted to do , but he'd do it just for the hell of it, he was just one of those people, uncontrollable, he was like a wild stallion …there was no way you could do anything with him, if you tried to put a saddle on he'd bite you, he was a genius, a hell of a talent, but like all geniuses he had a couple of flakes missing, he wanted to go on and do things but he didn't know what, and it made him so frustrated he just hit out'.

Alan Wheeler was Johnny Kidd and The Pirates manager but in the short time he worked with Dickie he did everything he possibly could for him to no avail, it seemed as if the whole recording industry was against him, and Alan for trying,

Dickie at this time was still saying that he didn't want to do Rock and Roll anymore, which in its self was a problem because Alan Wheeler could get work for him singing Rock and Roll at a lot of venues for a lot of clients, but he wasn't having any of it,

It's strange because Dickie could have got himself into the limelight and probably a recording contract performing Rock and Roll and then would have been able to change the music from the inside,

 as it were, but Dickie wasn't prepared to sing Rock and Roll. So, the option was not open to him.

Dickie was a musical snob in some respects, but this was probably down to his musical upbringing, he didn't like pop and didn't like jazz very much anymore,

his only compromise was an audition that Alan Wheeler had set up for him for Associated Rediffusion Television at their Kingsway Studios,

 the same studios that 'Ready Steady Go' was recorded at; they were looking for two permanent vocalists for a television series called 'Stars And Garters'.

Dickie auditioned for this at the Kingston studios and had decided to approach this audition from a middle of the road angle,

he sang 'Time and a River' an old Nat King Cole number that he had featured on his first 'Rock and Trad Spectacular' And had gone down really well with the audience,

and 'Isn't This a Lovely Day' and There's a small hotel tracks off his album *'Pride Without Prejudice'*

which was released on Columbia Records, all accompanied with just a piano to provide the music.

The A and R men were very pleased with Dickie's performance,

but he didn't get the contract because the producers had decided that they wanted someone who sang music that was a bit more up tempo, as in the current vein.

It went to Tommy Bruce and Gary Miller, and the female leads were Kathy Kirby and Lynn Cornell, the show was a big hit at the time,

Kathy Kirby was the only one to have had a hit by this time, so Dickie wouldn't have been out of place and probably would have done an equally good job,

and it would have revitalized Dickie's career which is just what he needed at this time.

Dickie was now living with Duffy Power, and he was starting to get into drugs in a big way, because everything was starting to go wrong, his marriage was finally over,

no one was interested in his music anymore, and he couldn't understand how it was that the new wave of musicians were playing the same music as he did, singing the same songs and were a success, but he wasn't.

he found it difficult to appreciate that an entirely different audience had grown up and to them he came from a different era,

which was a different world to them, Duffy Power and Marty Wilde did adapt briefly, and they switched to the 'new' style of music, and both released great singles that did quite well, Duffy Power released a R and B single called

'It Ain't Necessarily So' and Marty Wilde released an R and B single called 'Lonely Avenue' but nobody saw that this was a field that Dickie would potentially be great at.

One of the biggest exes Parnes performers did come out of this era Georgie Fame,

who went on to have lots of hits with his new sound,

Georgie Fame was a good friend of Dickie's, and he used to look up to him when they both worked for Larry Parnes,

he was only sixteen at the time

Dickie would refuse to take a rock 'n' roll booking, he was doing his best to lose the 'sheik of shake' image,

Dickie had a bad reputation in the business he could become aggressive at the drop of a hat.

a few bookings were coming in for rock 'n' roll gigs, but Dickie would not hear of it.

"I couldn't break him into the field he wanted to perform in Due to his past reputation, it was a stand-off situation.

Although I knew he was heavily dependent on the drug scene

his death in 1969 was a shock and a sad loss, a little while later Alan Wheeler went over to see

Dickies mother who had moved into an old people flat just down the road from the house Billy Fury and Joe Brown had once been put up overnight,

'I presented her with a copy of Dickie's LP, and she was pleased to have a copy again,

She showed me a nice letter that she had received from Billy Fury and one from Joe Brown, After Dickies death,

 he even mentioned staying with her at 43 Heathfield Avenue Selsdon South Croydon.

Mrs Kneller showed me a photograph of Dickie with Billy Fury taken in a restaurant in Croydon not too long before his death.in 1968 both of them were visibly ill Billy in the grip of the heart disease that would eventually kill him, Dickie had grown a long beard and had not long gotten over a serious head operation.

Dickie got involved with the Sidewinders again as they were the closest kind of music to what Dickie wanted to sing, from this performance they were invited to audition for the support spot for the very young Stevie Wonder show on his forthcoming British tour.

So, on a Sunday morning the band appeared at the Marquee Club in London with various other bands, Auditions and rehearsals were held to provide accompaniment to a very young Stevie Wonder on his next British tour

the Sidewinders were very successful and got the job much to the chagrin of the other bands who had made an effort and got dressed in their best stage clothes, they went through their selections of their repertoire while an extremely official MD from Tamla Motown politely rejected them one at a time until the last collection of musicians who had looked like they had just fallen out of bed stumbled onto the stand and the sidewinders were scruffy by comparison, but the Sidewinders got the job, there were some loud protests from the smartly dressed musicians in the audience but as was pointed out by the MD from Tamla Motown that's suits and slick hair do's don't get the job done

But they were picked because of their talent not because of the way they looked.

Roger Arthur a fan said,

Dickie played in the interval at the flamingo in 1965 in the west end supporting Screaming Jay Hawkins, his hair was Parted, and he sang 'Walking the dog',

during a ten minute or fifteen-minute set of mainly soul numbers he seemed pretty subdued, Tex Makins was also in the band backing him'. (Probably the Sidewinders).

1966

Sidewinders

Amyl Nitrate

Heroin

By this time Dickie was still only twenty-five he and his group the Sidewinders were able to get themselves booked as the support act with Stevie Wonder on a British tour.

who were very impressive but still didn't hit the big time,

they were still singing a lot of Jazz orientated songs, like 'Green Dolphin Street' Lullaby of Bird Land', 'Little Boy Don't Be Scared' and 'Parkers Mood' and many others,

he used to scat sing on stage, until he could think up some words,

Johnny Marshal the Saxophone player who was a heroin addict,

is remembered infamously as the man who turned Dickie onto Heroin, largely unintentionally though.

Despite his growing dependency on drugs especially Heroin he was now a user, and his career was the last thing on his mind, despite this he still completed a tour with Stevie Wonder who was 15 at the time, and on Monday the 7th of December he appeared with the sidewinders with Stevie Wonder at the Marque club, 90 Wardour street London W 1.

he also shared the bill with the Yard birds and The Animals.

The tour was

Jan 21st	the Flamingo Room London
Jan 22nd	the new all-star club London
Jan 22nd	Rhodes Club Bishops Stortford
Jan 23rd	Oasis Club Manchester
Jan 26th	Orchid Ballroom Purley
Jan 27th	Clevermead Windsor
Jan 28th	Mister Mc Coys Middlesbrough
Jan 29th	Old Hill Plaza Old Hill

Jan 30th   The Flamingo room London
Feb 3rd   Cedar Club Birmingham
Feb 4th   Dominic Club Manchester
Feb5th   Cue Club London
Feb 6th   Dungeon Club Nottingham
Feb 7th   St Joseph's Hall Basingstoke
Feb 23rd   Top ten Club Belle Vue, Manchester

Boz Burrell said 'the band were good, but it was disorganised,'

'The last time the band were reunited was in late 1966 performing as Jimmy Scott's O bladee O bladda Band at the Orchid Ballroom in Putney nearly every one of the band turned up except Tex Makins and Boz Burrell who had other commitments,

Those that turned up were Marc Penn, Boots Slade, Len Neldrett, Dickie Pride and Jimmy? on conga's

Dickie was great he was still on form the hall was pretty full, who says miracles can't happen, that was the end of the story,

the band went their separate ways and that was it'.

'The Next Thing I heard Dickie was with the Cyril Stapleton band and he was using heroin regularly'.

Jazz Musicians in the 1960's jumped from the jazz clubs to the pop scene,

an example was Chris Barber, granted they brought with them some excellent music,

and obviously if this was the way to go so be it, it was a way for musicians to make ends meet, but they didn't like it because in their eyes they were selling out,

but it had to be done, and it meant more people would get to hear their music.

Unfortunately, they also brought the drug culture with them,

Jazz musicians had been using drugs for years,

But they had also been having casualties for years.

Dickie was to become another casualty,

Becoming, the first Rock and Roll casualty of Heroin Addiction. And of the Rock n Roll lifestyle associated with it.

As gigs started to fall away and life got a bit more difficult, the Drugs that Dickie started to use become harder, it was during this year that Dickie moved on to the harder class of drug, Heroin, at a party and quickly became addicted, this was eventually going to kill him.

At this time, it was fairly rare to be a heroin addict, there was only 600 registered users in the whole of the UK.

They had their own culture and pick up points, with more addicts either ending up dead or in a psychiatric ward for Drug abuse, Dickie used to get his Methadone fix at the all-night pharmacy in Piccadilly

Tex Makins recalls

"Dickie would try anything; I remember once we were playing at 'the Marquee' as the 'Sidewinders'

Dickie and I were having a drink at the bar after having a joint outside in the gig wagon, when Georgina Shaw, who was their manager at the time,

came up to us and said that she had some liquid meth (speed), we said

"Great, lets drink it then",

it was a small brown tablet bottle, there was the equivalent of about six or seven phials of Methradrine in it,

a phial contained about a teaspoon; we didn't inject it we drank it.

Georgina emptied the bottle into a bottle of coke, and we drank the lot between the three of us, surprise surprise, it wasn't Meth it was acid (LSD),

in those days acid was sold on sugar cubes, 3 or 4 drops on each cube so you can imagine the state we were in"

it's suspected that Dickie got deeper and deeper into drugs and whatever money he was making was going on drugs, Dickie was into Amyl nitrate, a drug that was used to revive heart attack patients and amphetamines, which he used to inject,

one day taking the needle and just ramming the needle into his legs through the trousers, Dickie used to say Duffy wasn't a proper user because he wouldn't do this.

Dickie was spotted working with the Don Lang Band at the Cats Whiskers club in Streatham which used to be the Locarno.

He was also seen working for a band called the Olson Rolson band, in North London, it wasn't long after this that Dickie had a nervous breakdown and ended up in the mental hospital

His Sister Ann said:

He disappeared for a year we just didn't see him, then one day he came home looking like a Rabbi he had a long black beard and long black hair he looked absolutely awful he'd come back home to confess that he was on Heroin, we were absolutely devastated. He had spent most of 1966 getting deeper into the drug scene and had become actively addicted.

It was After about four years Dickie decided to visit his old Girlfriend Mandy (Madelyn Jocelyn) who was now married and called Mandy Atkinson,

who had to have been his closest friend while he was growing up,

Mandy said "one day he just turned up again,

 I just opened the door and there he was, it was something I'd always wondered about, we always knew what each other were doing, he looked haggard and he'd grown much taller, he told me about drugs and told me he could no longer find a vein,

he'd changed, when I last saw him, we were teenagers, now he 'd become a man, and I was married with two children".

this wasn't the last time Mandy saw Dickie by any means and Dickie didn't forget her' he counted on their relationship and friendship a few months later,

when he needed her support to get through the revolutionary new treatment that Dickie was to undertake to help cure him of his addiction to Heroin.

Dickie returned home to his mums and sister who was living with her when he got there, they were shocked he was desperate for help to cure his addiction,

his family got him to seek medical advice Because he had now realised that he needed help with his heroin addiction

Mandy got a phone call from a hospital asking her to go to the hospital and help support Dickie, as support was necessary for him to undergo some revolutionary treatment, she used to take a taxi up to the hospital twice a week and take her children with her,

he used to say that if things were different the children could have been his.

If Dickie was feeling down or called,

she would go to the Hospital or later to the flat, she wasn't in love with him but there was a tremendous bond of affection and loyalty between the two of them,

They had known each other for so long, they had been through so much together that this thread would never be broken between them,

Even after Dickie's death.

He seemed to think he was worth nothing,

When he came out of hospital he returned to his mother's flat,

She was now living in old persons flat, there were still the faint echoes of fame around him and all his friends would buy him a drink at the legion

With help from psychiatrists at the Chelsea Drug Addiction Centre and the hospital, he was able to kick the habit for about two years.

At Dickie's inquest it was said that he had managed to stay away from drugs for about two years but had gone back to them just before he died

This was probably 1967, 1968 so it's highly likely that during 1966 he got deeper, and deeper into drugs and was actively involved.

Dickie tried to sing Swing, big band jazz, R+B, Latin, Jazz rhythms and anything else he could sing he was great at all of them but couldn't find a niche for him to sing in

but he was certain he didn't want to sing rock 'n' roll

Although he was great at it, he did not find it challenging enough for him.

Duffy Said 'Dickie was a musical snob, he hated pop, and he didn't really like the blues but towards the end of his career he began to get into complex Latin American rhythms, and he sounded so great it was frightening'

1967

Nervous breakdown

Leucotomy

Back home to mum

It wasn't long after this that Dickie had a nervous breakdown, Dickie's mood swings and violent outbursts were put down to pressure on the brain caused by either a blood clot, or his skull pressing on his brain.

Dickie could not keep up his non-use of heroin, so his doctors had him entered a psychiatric hospital for treatment,

It was eventually decided that he could be cured with a leucotomy (lobotomy). he was referred to The Brook Hospital, a mental hospital. Despite having a young baby Ricky, Dickie split up with his wife Tricia who later moved to the United States, he moved back home with his mother, then living in Tedder road Selsdon and he joined a rehabilitation programme, where he was given Methadone and he attended a therapy group, for a while he was admitted to the Nethern mental hospital and then on to the Chelsea drug clinic. But his depression got worse because of his drug addiction, and it was recommended that he undergo a leucotomy (a lobotomy) the thinking at that time was drug addiction was caused by depression, cure the depression and this will cure the addiction to drugs and all of his other problems would go away, unfortunately the only way to cure serious depression was to give the patient a Leucotomy where the white nerve fibres in the frontal lobes of the brain are severed the connection of the frontal cortex with the other parts of the nervous system especially the Thalamus and Hypothalamus is cut that involved opening up a person's skull and cutting out a piece of his brain. This barbaric operation is usually carried out on people with severe depression or are very obsessive, this operation seems to work and it relieves the symptoms, the person becomes more responsive, cheerful and more relaxed and more agreeable and interested in what is going on around them And one of the reasons for his depression was put down to the fact that Parnes would not let Dickie sing the songs that he wanted to, only letting him sing Rock n Roll, he wanted to sing Cole Porter, Gershwin, Rogers and Hart,

Billy Fury got round this problem by writing his own songs, Dickie's artistic block meant that Dickie was left Stewing in frustration which contributed to his mental decline Dickie's mood changes and violence was put down to pressure on the brain caused by either his skull pressing on his brain or a blood clot because he was so violent the Leucotomy was decided on

The operation went ahead, and they inserted Radioactive seeds into the frontal cortex of his brain this will cure the addiction and also the depression and it seemed to have worked, for almost a year after he returned to his old self. After the operation He was a different man.

According to Duffy:

'Dickies operation did Dickie a lot of good, I saw Dickie about four months before he died and he looked great, I thought you've cracked it, this man can go anywhere he had got Dickie Kneller sorted out and I felt sort of envious, he was relaxed he was sitting in a chair properly for the first time ever and he talked about his future about projects, he become human, I felt that he had come back to reality after all these years'.

When he found out about Dickies death, he realised that maybe he could have helped Dickie a bit more, he did say that if Dickie had lived there is a good chance that he and Dickie would have worked together and who knows what might have happened with Dickie's career, but Dickie was a hard guy to please at the time.

Duffy was going through a drug problem of his own with Amphetamines he withdrew, and he spent a lot of money on Psychiatrists, thankfully he was able to sort himself out and became one of the 20th centuries greatest bluesmen.

The thinking behind this operation at that time was by then out of date and was rarely being used.

it was well past it's sell by date even then.

But this operation doesn't always work, and the effects wear off in time and the patient returns to the way they were.

To be honest though it is not surprising really, as he would be too scared of this being done to him again.

Psychiatrists today would recognize Dickie's behavioural problems as a symptom of acute shock,

in this case the death of his father, while he was very young,

Often rendering the sufferer as incapable of normal communication

and prone to sudden outburst of either verbal or physical violence when under stress,

But in those days, he was simply seen as a 'nutter',

he certainly would not have to undergo a brain operation today.

Dickie was unfortunate because he was one of the first Rock and roll singers to become addicted to Heroin.

Duffy Power put it very well when he said that "if Elton John had had his addiction in the early 1960's he would have been dead as well,

He's alive now because of the help and back up there is for him now,

but Dickie had to cope alone, and nobody can do that,

You can only hurt people so many times before they turn their backs on you".

The Leucotomy was performed at the Brook Hospital,

it was a strange thing to do, an irreversible operation on someone so young,

It is believed that the depression was caused by his wife leaving him,

but it's more likely that it was initially the death of his father that had something to do with it,

Dickie was only twenty-four. At this time

The family was told that they had planted radioactive seeds in his brain (this may have been to burn off some cells).

The family had always assumed that the operation was to cure Dickie's drug addiction, but it was done to cure his violent tendencies.

At first the operation had seemed to work and do him some good,

he was a different man; he improved considerably,

although he had stopped singing by this time

By the end of 1967 He was able to find work away from show business and found work as a lorry driver for a firm in Addington,

'He was very proud that he could park his big van and drive it so well',

The operation had calmed him down and he is thought to have definitely benefited,

But it wasn't long before Dickie was taking heroin again.

After Dickie had his operation, it took him a long time to recover and he was in a pretty poor state,

but in a chance meeting with Duffy Power,
Duffy said that he was surprised by how well he
was looking, thinking

'This man has cracked it, this man can go
somewhere, he'd got Dickie Kneller sorted out
and I felt envious, he was relaxed, he was sitting
in a chair properly for the first time ever

and talked about the future, and about projects,
he'd become human, I'd felt he had come back
to reality after all these years".

1968

Margaret Simmons

Meeting Billy Fury

Depression

But by 1968 he was fit enough and able enough
to meet some of the people that knew him and
his mother,

who he always returned to if he was in trouble.

The relationship between Dickie and his mother was intense and occasionally stormy.

They always needed each other and reassured each other,

they did argue and hurt each other, and His mother also had a temper on her

But he did cause her a lot of pain

But he always went back to her, he, was said to have popped Amyl nitrate under her nose on one occasion.

Dickie's sister hit him over the head with a shoe once because she thought that he was attacking his mum,

Dickie did try to curb his temper on many occasions but to no avail sadly.

He broke his mum's finger once; he was sorry about it but by that time he was too late.

He was well enough to visit his mother's old folks club,

although at this time he had grown a long beard,

The old folk there still counted him as a famous person and were always buying him drinks

Dickie visited his old girlfriend Margaret Simmons who of course was now married, they started dating in 1958 but she called it off because he was always going to the studio and she wanted someone who wanted to settle down and have a family which she didn't think that Dickie would do because he was too involved with his music, they stayed friends and when she did marry and have kids, he came round

he took her two sons out, who he knew very well,

she did have second thoughts because he was obviously on drugs,

but in the end, she let him,

he took them out in his lorry and when he returned them, he had brought them loads of stuff,

He kissed Margaret to say goodbye and she started to cry, because she couldn't believe how bad he had become because of the drugs.

One and a half years later he was found dead of a massive drugs overdose, when she found out she said that it was such a waste from someone who was so talented and so young just 27 years of age.

Hal Carter also remembered bumping into him outside the John Gunnel Agency, he was sporting a small Spanish style beard and was dressed like a beatnik,

with sandals, no socks, and trousers hanging off him half-mast and he was wearing a big overcoat,

he looked ill and was a very ill man by this time.

Dickie also met up with Duffy Power whom he told about his time in the psychiatric hospital and his operation

he had told Duffy about some of the people he had met while in there and Duffy said that Dickie sounded really human.

Dickies uncontrollable temper outbursts today would be seen as a symptom of shock i.e.

the death of his father,

which after rendering the sufferer to be incapable of normal communication and capable of sudden uncontrollable outbursts of verbal and physical violence and would be treated with the right means of treatment to control it

Being seen as ill

In the '60's he was just seen as a nutter and couldn't be trusted'.

He attended an outpatient clinic at South Norwood and also one at the Northern hospital drugs unit which was close to his home.

Hal Carter Said ' I think myself that there was something terribly wrong in his childhood,

but I don't know what it was.

He had a hell of a talent, he could sing anything, and he could dance, play piano, guitar, anything really, I would say he was a genius with a couple of flakes missing.

the trouble was he was completely uncontrollable and violent, when he drank, he didn't just get drunk he got unconscious and he was into drugs early on right from the start,

as well as drinking

he thought that twelve bars of rock and roll was shit he wanted to be an all-round entertainer but the only thing that they would let him do was rock and roll because that is how Parnes made money out of him,

the only way he could get on television was to do' Slippin and Slidin' and he was very frustrated as a performer.

He was a genius who wanted to do things,

but he didn't know about himself, except that it was something different,

He wouldn't argue with you he'd just hit out; he'd lay you out,

he couldn't stand having things done any way but his own,

they say hit first and talk afterwards in Dickie's case there wasn't any talking'.

Dickie met up with Billy Fury by accident at the end of 1968 and they had dinner together at a Croydon restaurant they were seen sitting next to each other in a grey ford Zephyr car which came speeding along gravel hill, it pulled to a halt, backed up and then screeched off into the distance, it was not long after that according to Penelope Sutherland Young (nee Le Clair) that Dickie had died of an overdose

Dickie and Billy both had great talent musically, if they had both survived to today who knows what they could have both achieved.

As solo acts in their own rights or as a fantastic collaboration of the two of them.

together they could probably have given Lennon and McCartney a run for their money.

Dickie met Billy Fury in November 1958 and the two of them became firm friends,

from the beginning Billy became Dickies closest friend and protector from Larry Parnes stopping Parnes from Sacking Dickie On a few occasions.

Insisting after Parnes had sacked him that Dickie should be brought back to tour with him, after Billy's heart problems started to interfere in his performances Where Dickie would go on for him., when he was too ill to perform.

Dickie did make attempts at writing his own music he said in court that he was doing so,

he was one of the few who could read and write music, but it looks like none of his music has survived.

While Dickie was Experimenting with Jazz and Latin music which he found was uncommercial, even though his efforts were brilliant,

His fondness for drugs and drink meant it was impossible to concentrate on writing new music, he was usually under the influence of something, making him loud, aggressive, and wild and also humorous, despite Billy Fury's Efforts to save Dickie from himself, he was unable to do so,

and Dickie went to an early grave.

Whereas Billy was a warm gentle shy quiet person,

they were like the two faces of the same coin, getting on so well together, as they both saw things in each other that they would like to be

Like yin and yang.

Dickie was also attending a drug unit as an outpatient at South Norwood

and receiving treatment at the Nethern Hospital, he was on Methadone to help him with his addiction

and he was taking Mandrax to help him sleep, nothing else.

Dickie had managed to stay away from heroin for two years 1967 and 1968 and had pledged to keep away from drugs altogether.

but the depression was taking a hold again,

he found it very difficult to accept that at one time he would be dragged up to sing at any party or function and the next thing he was a forgotten man,

No one was interested in him anymore.

he was also depressed when he thought that now his old girlfriend was married and had two kids, it could have been his life.

Dickie returned to his mum's house and was virtually unable to get work as a singer.

But he did get some work.

1969
Yellow Submarine Club
Heroin and Mandrax
Death

For a while Dickie had control of his habit but he couldn't resist his old haunts in jazz cellars and bars where his old mates were still part of the drug scene.

He was soon visiting them again and mixing with the wrong kind of people that an ex-addict shouldn't be associating with.

On 26th of March Dickie told his doctor that he had started taking drugs again and had been using Heroin again

Dickie was unable to resists the temptation a couple of times,

It was pointed out by his doctor that it was very dangerous for an ex-addict to return to drugs again. The chance of developing a real addiction is higher.

On One Occasion his sister Ann came downstairs in the night to find Dickie searching through his mother's drugs cabinet,

getting out all the medicines searching for a strong drug to take,

'There was a kind of Desperation about him' she said,

'I can't help but think what would have happened if he had been one of today's stars with all the help, they have available,

Robbie Williams has spoken about being right to the brink and back,

my brother went to the brink and fell off".

Earlier on in this year Dickie started to make a comeback as a singer, he was feeling well enough

And on March 24th he visited his old Girlfriend Mandy Atkinson to have his hair cut it had grown so long, he also had a beard.

after his old band the Sidewinders had disbanded,

Johnny Marshal, Ray Mills (Alan Price's ex drummer) Dickie, Bob Steele (ex-playboys and Johnny Halliday) and Tex Makins had formed a band with Dickie as lead vocalist the band which didn't have a name as they hadn't got around to naming,

They were the resident band at The Yellow Submarine club in the basement of the Royal Lancashire Hotel,

they had played for the last fortnight and were starting to sound great but on the night of the 24th Dickie didn't show, and they carried on without a vocalist,

The next night, he didn't show up again,

It was found out three weeks later that Dickie had died.

On the 24th He left his mother's house to go to the Yellow Submarine club in London to perform,

but he met an old colleague, a Saxophone player from the Cyril Stapleton band and an ex-heroin user,

called John Peter King, who lived in Buford Garden in Chelsea,

He used to be a heroin user but according to him he was practically cured?

As he was now happily married,

He and Dickie went to get some prescriptions from a chemist, and then they went back to Peter Kings flat for a meal.

Peter King told the Coroner at Dickie's inquest that

'He had put some drugs including Heroin, which he had collected, into his bathroom'.

(Of course, a man who was 'cured' would not have any drugs in his bathroom, just because of the temptation, he was probably still addicted, and may have not been telling the truth),

And sometime during that evening Dickie took heroin again,

which he probably got from Peter Kings bathroom, after a meal and a nice evening Dickie went home on the bus.

When he returned home that evening, he told his mother he wasn't feeling well and went to bed.

This was the reason that he didn't turn up for his gig at the Yellow Submarine club on the 24th.

Dickie stayed in bed for that day and most of the next two days

On the Tuesday morning Dickie's brother Bob who was a fireman, and his friend Keith Wonham were driving past Dickie's mums house in a fire engine when they were waved down by Bob and Dickie's mum,

they went to investigate what was wrong, when they got into the house, they found Dickie overdosed on the settee,

They carried him upstairs to his bedroom, they wanted to call a doctor, but Dickie's mum wouldn't hear of it,

so, they left him lying in his bed.

He had been unable to eat, and spent the next two days, the 24th and 25th mainly, in bed.

he did leave his house on the 25th the night before he died, though.

Even though he was feeling ill, he wanted to get out of the house for a while, so he went for a drink, He bumped into an old friend called Arthur Grey, whom he had a drink with at the Tamworth Arms, Tamworth Road, Croydon,

They arranged to meet up the next night to have another drink. But Arthur Couldn't get there, that was the day that Dickie had been found dead.

Arthur Grey was probably the last person to see Dickie alive.

On the 26th, his mother went into his room and tried to wake him up, when she couldn't she phoned for an ambulance, it was too late

She found him dead in his bed.

Mandy Atkinson received a phone call from the vicar of St Francis'. Church saying that Mrs Kneller had died, Mandy wasn't there but the message was taken by an au pair,

When she got the message, she had been going to visit Mrs Kneller,

Whom she was a great friend of,

When she got a phone call again from the vicar who then told her that Dickie had died,

She was stunned and spent the next two days walking around like a zombie.

She was very upset that it had also been reported that Dickie had committed suicide

And it still bothers her now that people would think so,

She says:

When Dickie sang nothing else mattered to him he was magnetic on stage, no one went to the toilet when he was singing he was definitely charismatic he had a voice that would make your toes curl, she thought that it would go on forever, he would sing all his songs to her from the stage, just the two of them know about that but eventually he became someone she didn't know, he didn't sing Eddie Cochran because he knew Eddie and toured with him up until the day he died but he did sing a lot of Buddy Holly, his favourite songs were

That'll be the day, Great balls of fire, long tall Sally, Heartbreak Hotel, When I fall in love (Nat King Cole), Peggy Sue and anything else by Buddy Holly'.

Tex Makins was under the impression that Dickie didn't simply die of an overdose and t that Dickie had died in his bed and had burnt to death thereafter, the bed had caught fire because he was smoking in it and was incapacitated because of his drug addiction he was unable to escape from it. And that is where he died.

Everything points to his death being a very tragic accident and miscalculation on Dickie's part.

Mandy's opinion on Dickie's drug taking was that

"he was led into it by people who said

'Take this will help you sleep'. 'This will keep you awake', it's just like taking a drink',

I don't see any other way that he would have got into it, he was easily led,

I think he probably started doing it when he met Lionel Bart and that lot.

he used to tell me about drugs, he told me he used some that kept him on the loo with diarrhoea that sounded like fun

when he came back from hospital, he was off Heroin but was on Methadone

but he was admitted to a mental hospital

At one time he probably got into drugs thinking, 'this is something new I'll try it".

She says that Dickie was

'a gentle man, fun loving, always laughing and with a ready smile, he had a sympathetic and enquiring mind, he was an intelligent man, there is no doubt about that,

But Sometimes when Dickie and Mandy argued Dickie would say

'I'll kill myself' but he never meant it.

Eventually he became someone I didn't know'

There is no evidence that Dickie meant to kill himself, and all available evidence says that this is the case...

Dickie's mother told the court that her son had been making a good recovery during the past two years

But he had not been feeling well ever since the Monday night,

At the inquest at Croydon on April 30th, 1969, Dickie's recorded verdict was 'Barbiturate poisoning, Death from Addiction to drugs.

This was probably due to the sleeping tablets that he had been taking to help him sleep, probably because he couldn't sleep after taking the Heroin.

he took more tablets than he should have, and he never woke up,

during the evening of the 26th he also took his usual dose of Mandrax to help him sleep, in his confused state he may have forgotten that he had taken his Mandrax, and he may have taken it again to help him sleep.

The postmortem also revealed that there were puncture marks on his arm, estimated to be about two days old,

A Doctor Henry Dale Beckett, a consultant psychiatrist who had treated Dickie,

told the inquest that Dickie had suffered acute depression over the breakup of his marriage.

he had attended the Chelsea Drug Addiction Centre,

where he was cured of drug use and had kept clean of them for the last two years.

Doctor Beckett told the inquest that Dickie had admitted to being tempted over the last month and had started taking drugs again,

The coroner Doctor Mary McHugh said,

"I am certain that this young man did not intend to take his own life,

he was depressed, but the evidence is that he was becoming a lot happier".

At the first inquest held on the 2nd of April but had been adjourned Dr Mary Mc Hugh commented at that inquest into Richards passing that he seemed to have coped well with his difficulties and had all but surmounted them only to suffer a tragic relapse, he had, she said been depressed, but the evidence seemed to indicate that he had become a lot happier'.

The Pathologist Dr David Bowen said,

"The cause of death was Barbiturate poisoning, the level of drugs in his blood was far above a level which would indicate a therapeutic dose', he had found several old puncture wounds in his skin, on his arm and had also found one that could not have been more than two days old.

The coroner said.

'I am certain that this young man did not mean to take his life, he had been depressed but the evidence shows that he was becoming a lot happier'

His verdict, death from addiction to drugs.

At the time of Dickie's death, he was written down as having no occupation, and his address was number 6 Tedder Road, South Croydon,

 this was the address of his mums and was an old person flat.

Dickies death attracted lots of coverage in the press, but the interest was in his drug addiction, when Dickie died Billy Fury sent Mrs. Kneller a very nice letter regretting his death as did Joe Brown,

She was adamant that Dickie's death was not a drugs overdose,

 and that he had beaten his drug addiction, and he was more like himself.

Dickie's funeral made no headlines at the time, and there was a small family funeral,

 his sister Ann Said

'We didn't advertise it at the time, anyway. By then he had stopped being Dickie Pride and was just plain Richard Kneller. I can't help but think what would have happened if he had been one of today's stars with all the help, they have available Robbie Williams has spoken about being right to the brink and back, my brother went to the brink and fell off'

Alan Wheeler who was one of Dickie's managers visited Dickie's mum after his death and presented her with Dickie's album,

she was thrilled to have it again,

and she was still adamant that Dickie had not died of an overdose, she showed him Billy Fury's letter.

Duffy Power Said about Dickie,

'Dickie Pride was violent, lazy and devious, at the same time he was affable, very funny, lovable and at the age of eighteen was a major vocal talent in Great Britain, had he lived he would have achieved sooner or later the recognition he deserved,

he was very special'.

When the documentary Parnes, Shilling and pence was aired,

Dickie's mum was thrilled by Joe browns tribute to Dickie.

Dickie's wife was at the funeral and so was his mum and sister unfortunately, there was no contact between her and Dickies mother,

There were very few others at the funeral.

Dickie Pride or Richard Kneller was cremated at Croydon Crematorium on the 3rd of April 1969.

Not long after Dickie died his brother died, (December 1969),

Dickie's brother, who was a fireman, died of a heart attack brought on by cancer, while he was at work,

This devastated Dickie's mum and his sister.

His friend Keith Wonham said

'Bob was pretty fit, was a fireman and used to play football.

he had just moved from Grinstead and was stationed at Croydon fire station,

It was nine in the morning, and he just keeled over,

he was taken to Croydon intensive care unit, but he died there.

Keith was there and so was Bob's wife.

Apparently, Mrs Kneller knew Dickie's son Ricky and kept in touch by visiting him in America,

Richard Junior is the spitting image of his dad, and he still lives in America. And is called Richard Ludt.

Unfortunately he committed suicide in 2011 aged 46 at Portland Oregon by jumping off Fremont bridge on October the 11 after months of severe depression his body was recovered and identified two days later.

And Dickies ex-wife Patricia Ludt died in America of an Alzheimer's related illness on April 11th, 2014, after a sixteen year battle with Alzheimer's disease, after Dickies death she met Rudolph Ludt ,married and they moved to New York they had a daughter Muriel.

Dickies mum regretted Dickie was ever discovered as a pop singer as he did not make the grade she thought.

In 1984:

Dickie performed at the big star show in Liverpool in 1960 and was seen by a 13 year old Paul McCartney he was impressed by Dickie and said on a radio interview for Radio London in 1984 that it was Dickie's act and voice that remained with him to that day, he said of all of the acts on that show that night he especially remembered Dickie Pride and loved his voice this is where he heard him sing 'Ain't she Sweet' the Beatles later recorded this number while they were in Germany because of it'.

In November 1997 at the AGM of the John Newnham Association (Dickies old school), they released a fantastic 5 page tribute to their former pupil Richard Charles Kneller ie Dickie Pride, which described his rise to singing with the country's greatest pop empresario's Larry Parnes' stable of Stars, with a great description of Richard and describes how as a ten year old pupil used to keep his fellow pupils enthralled by his musical numbers, it also goes on to document his win at various talent contests for his singing and his well-earned place at the Royal School of church music as a chorister and his rise to fame on various TV Shows such as Oh Boy, and billed as the sheik of Shake and his success in the charts with Primrose Lane, although he is best remembered for his wonderful version of Little Richard's Slippin and Slidin it also mentioned that he never quiet reached the heights that his contemporaries

Marty Wilde and Cliff Richard were to attain, and the regret at aged 27 in 1969 of the loss of a man whom they all remembered as the happy go lucky youngster who kept his school friends entertained with his rendition of Johnny Ray's 'Cry', 'The little white cloud that cried' and look homeward Angel'.

This tribute was obviously written by someone who remembers Richard well. And says that he is someone who will indeed be remembered with 'Pride' not only by his school mates but also by all of those who heard and enjoyed his music,

and because his records have gone on to be collectors' items,

in that respect Dickie Pride or Richard Kneller as the pupils of John Newnham school knew him as,

has achieved a sort of immortality.

His mother was in the Monks Hill British Legion, and she also used to sing in concerts entertaining old folk.

She died 20 years after Dickie.

Of course, the story does not end there, there are still people who are very interested in the Dickie Pride story,

people like me who love Dickie's voice and wants to know as much as possible about the man himself.

I am of the opinion that if I had known Dickie or Richard, I would have probably got on with him and I would have liked him I think that we could have been friends, who knows.

There are people like Charles Langley the playwright who was so intrigued by The Dickie Pride Story that he wrote and produced a successful play about Dickie that was performed in London.

Dickie Pride's son Rickie was still alive at that time, and he came over from Portland in Oregon to see the play and he had only come across it through the internet purely by chance.

Francis Stone who played Dickie Pride in the show said:

"We were all knocked out when we heard about it; it's a bit like having a ghost walk into the stalls,

At first, I felt slightly daunted at having the man's son watching me play his father but at least he would learn something about him and understand his extraordinary talent".

And of course, there are friends and colleagues of Dickie who knew the man and may want to know what happened to such a talented man and where it all went wrong.

The story does not end there though,

in July 2002 the BBC produced a series of programs called jukebox hero's'

 which were six half hour shows about great British Rock and Roll stars,

as the flyer said

'a new series of six 30-minute documentaries that take an intimate look at the flipside of Rock And Roll, the true and extraordinary stories of those pioneers who created British rock music from its beginnings'.

The others were Screaming Lord Sutch, John Leyton, Petula Clark, Bad finger, Ian Dury, and in its third program of the six, Dickie Pride,

 The program was produced by Paul Pierrot, who told me they were pleased with some of the material found for this program including the demo disc of Dickie singing 'I Go Ape'.

And there was the extract from the Saturday Club radio program unheard since the 1960's,

He was especially pleased with how clear the music was,

There were some wonderful photographs that had not been seen before by this author and a very familiar portrait of Dickie,

very familiar as I painted it!

Paul Pierrot did a great job of these shows, and it was a great timely reminder of Dickie's wonderful but underestimated talent.

With contributions from Marty Wilde, Duffy Power, Vince Eager and Georgie Fame among others. Who said

'I enjoyed working with Dickie more than any of the others including Billy Fury or Gene Vincent and he had a long way to go but unfortunately he cut it short'.

The last word has to come from Larry Parnes, whom Dickie had a love, hate relationship with a man who could have been the greatest influence in Dickie's life,

shocked by the news of Dickie's death remarked,

'when talent like his is wasted it is a crying shame this boy could have been a big star everybody said so',

"Dickie, poor Dickie, he died very young, but there was an Artiste, He made a wonderful album called *Pride without Prejudice*, which I named. He had a superb recording voice and stage act.

I remember Tommy Steele standing in the wings and saying, 'Boy, that fellow has got talent!"

Certainly, Dickie seemed to have the ability and potential to have carved out a much more successful career than he did.

Dickie Pride discography

Singles

1.

Slippin 'n' Slidin / don't make me love you
Columbia db. 4283 7 "UK 1959

2.

Slippin 'n' Slidin /don't make me love you
Columbia db. 4283 7"promo UK 1959

3.

Primrose Lane / Frantic 7" UK 1959
Columbia db. 4340

4.

Primrose Lane / Frantic 7" Germany 1959
Columbia C21 -307

5.

Primrose Lane / Frantic 7 Netherlands 1959
Columbia DB 4340

6.

Primrose Lane / Frantic 7" Norway 1959
Columbia DB 4340

7.

Slippin 'n' Slidin / Fabulous Cure 7" UK1959 Columbia DJ 4283

8.

Slippin 'n' Slidin / Fabulous Cure 7" UK1959 Columbia DJ4283

9

Midnight Oil / Fabulous Cure 7" UK 1959 Columbia DB4296

10.

You're Singing our love song to somebody else / Bye Bye Blackbird 7" UK 1960

Columbia DB 4451

11.

You're Singing Our Love Song to Somebody Else / Bye Bye Blackbird 7" Mono promo

Columbia DB 4451 UK 1960

12.

Betty Betty /No John 7" UK 1960

Columbia DB 4403

13.

When my little girl is smiling Jimmy Justice

Frantic Dickie Pride 7 "USA

Last Nite Records

14.

Slippin 'n' Slidin / Fabulous Cure UK 2009 Columbia DJ 4283 Demo record not for sale

15.

The Guvnors

Piccadilly TN 35117 (Bobby Shafto, Nelson Keene, Dickie Pride)

Let's Make a Habit of This/The Kissing Had to Stop April 1963

EP

1.

Dickie Pride the Sheik of Shake

Columbia SEG 7937 7" EP Mono UK 1959

Fabulous Cure, Slippin 'n' Slidin, Don't Make Me Love You, Midnight Oil

2.

Dickie Pride Primrose Lane France 1960

Columbia ESDF 1298 7" EP

Primrose Lane, Frantic, Slippin 'n' Slidin, Midnight Oil.

LP

Pride without Prejudice' LP 1960

LP 'Columbia Mono 335 x 1307

Stereo 3369

Tracks are: Anything Goes, It's Only A Paper Moon, Isn't It A Lovely Day, I Could Write A Book, You Turned The Tables On Me, Too Close For Comfort, Loch Lomond, There's A Small Hotel, Falling In Love, They Can't Take That Away From Me, Give Me A Simple Life, Lulu's Back In Town.

Dickie Pride was also known to record as the sound of Jimmy Nichol in 1965. Releasing a single on Decca F 12107 Entitled Clementine. /Bim Bam.

This is the only Track released by a Jimmy Nichol it's unsure if this is Dickie or not.

CD's

In 1992 a fabulous Compact Disc (Cd) was released on the 'see for miles 'label

Consisting of his entire A and B sides and all of the tracks from his album, an essential buy if you want to hear nearly all of Dickie's tracks:

1,

Dickie Pride See for miles See CD344 1992

Tracks are: Don't Make Me Love You, Slippin 'n' Slidin, Your Singing Our Love Song To Someone Else, Bye Bye Blackbird, Fabulous Cure, Midnight Oil, Betty Betty (Go Steady With Me), No John, Primrose Lane, Frantic, Anything Goes, It's Only A Paper Moon, Isn't This A Lovely Day, I Could Write A Book, You Turned The Tables On Me, Too Close For Comfort, Loch Lomond, There's A Small Hotel, Falling In Love, They Can't Take That Away From Me, Lulu's Back In Town.

2,

The complete Dickie Pride Peak soft PEA007

Tracks are: Slippin 'N' Slidin, Don't Make Me Love You, Fabulous Cure, Midnight Oil, Primrose Lane, Frantic, Betty Betty, No John, Bye Bye Blackbird, Your Singing Our Love Song To Someone Else, Give Me The Simple Life, Lulus Back In Town, Loch Lomond, Anything Goes, You Turned The Tables On Me, There's A Small Hotel, Falling In Love, They

Can't Take That Away, I Could Write A Book, Too Close For Comfort, Isn't This A Lovely Day, It's Only A Paper Moon, Let's Make A Habit Of This, The Kissing Had To Stop

3.

Blood Brothers The complete Dickie Pride Plus Billy Fury lost gems Peak soft PEA021

Tracks are: Slippin 'N ' Slidin, Don't Make Me Love You, Fabulous Cure, Midnight Oil, Primrose Lane, Frantic, Betty Betty, No John, Bye Bye Blackbird, Your Singing Our Love Song To Somebody Else, Give Me The Simple Life, Lulus Back In Town, Loch Lomond, Anything Goes, You Turned The Tables On Me , There's A Small Hotel, Falling In Love, They Can't Take That Away, I Could Write A Book, Too Close For Comfort, Isn't This A Lovely Day, It's Only A Paper Moon, Let's Make A Habit Of This, The Kissing Had To Stop,

Billy Fury bonus tracks: I Must Be Dreaming, In Thoughts of You, it's Only Make Believe, Break Up, Nobody's Child,

 My Life (Tony Diamond),

Love Don't Let Me Down (Johnny Storme).

4.

3 Cool Cats Cat Records

Cliff Richard, Marty Wilde and Dickie Pride. Double Album.

Tracks Are 3 Cool Cats featuring Cliff, Marty and Dickie, Anything Goes, Betty Betty, Bye Bye Blackbird, , Don't Make Me Love You, Fabulous Cure, Falling In Love, Frantic, Give Me The Simple Life, I could Write A book, Isn't This A Lovely Day, Loch Lomond, Lulus Back In Town, Midnight Oil, No John, Now's The Time To Fall In Love, Paper Moon, Primrose Lane, Slippin And Slidin, There's A Small Hotel, They Cannot Take That Away From Me, Too Close For Comfort, You Turned The Tables

On Me, Your Singing Our Love Song To Someone Else.

5.

Dickie Pride Slippin and Slidin RB Nostalgia 2015

Tracks are, Primrose Lane , Betty Betty Go Steady With Me, No John, It's Only A Paper Moon, Lu Lu's Back In Town, There's A Small Hotel, Anything Goes, They Can't Take That Away From Me, I Could Write A Book, Loch Lomond, You Turned The Tables On Me, Give Me The Simple Life, Falling In Love, Isn't This A Lovely Day, Too Close For Comfort, Bye Bye Blackbird, Midnight Oil, Slippin 'n' Slidin, Frantic, Don't Make Me Love You, Your Singing Our Love Song To Somebody Else.

6.

Dickie Pride, the Sheik of Shake Jasmine Records JASCD 1178, 2023.

Tracks are, Slippin' n Slidin', Don't Make Me Love You, Fabulous Cure, Midnight Oil, Primrose Lane, Frantic, Betty Betty (Go Steady With Me), No John, Your Singing Our Love Song To Someone Else,, Bye Bye Blackbird,

Anything Goes, It's Only A Paper Moon, Isn't this a Lovely Day, I Could Write A Book, You Turned The Tables On Me, Too Close for Comfort, Loch Lomond, There's a Small Hotel, Falling in Love, They Can't Take That Away From Me, Give Me The Simple Life, Lulu's Back In Town, Bonus Tracks, Slippin n Slidin live, Three Cool Cats (with Marty Wilde and Cliff Richard).

Also in Existence is a demo disc of Dickie singing 'Such a Night' recorded in 1957.

Also in Existence is another demo disc of Dickie singing 'I Go Ape' which was featured and heard for the first time on the Television documentary Jukebox Heroes in 2002.

Dickie recorded 'Out of Sight' along with three other unknown tracks for Joe Meek with a view to releasing,

This hasn't seen the light of day since its recording in 1965.

Dickie recorded a demo disc at the Morden Recording Studios in 1965, the two tracks recorded were 'Out Of Sight' and 'Get on the Right Track Baby'

Dickie Pride A to Z
(Every track and where to find it)

A

Anything Goes

(Porter)

LP Pride without Prejudice. CD Dickie Pride the Sheik of Shake, CD Slippin 'n' Slidin With Dickie Pride, CD The Complete Dickie Pride, Dickie Pride the Shiek Of Shake Blood Brothers, CD Three Cool Cats. CD Dickie Pride Slippin and Slidin.

Ain't She Sweet

(Dickie Performed This at the Liverpool Empire on the Big Star Show)

B

Bye Bye Blackbird

(Dixon Henderson)

B Side 45, B Side 45 Mono Promo, LP Pride Without Prejudice Dickie Pride the Sheik Of Shake, CD Slippin 'n' Slidin With Dickie Pride, CD The Complete Dickie Pride, CD Blood Brothers, CD Three Cool Cats. CD Dickie Pride Slippin and Slidin. CD Dickie Pride the Sheik of Shake,

Bye Bye Blackbird

(Dixon Henderson)

Sung on the Television Program, Riverboat Shuffle in 1961.

Betty Betty (Go Steady With Me)

(Ross Barry, Peter Morris)

A Side 45, LP Pride Without Prejudice, CD Dickie Pride the Sheik Of Shake, CD Slippin 'n' Slidin With Dickie Pride, CD The Complete Dickie Pride, CD Blood Brothers, CD Three Cool Cats. CD Dickie Pride Slippin and Slidin.CD Dickie Pride the Sheik of Shake.

C

Cry

(Churchill Kohlman)

(Was Sung in the Washroom of John Newnham School for a Bunch of His Friends)

Cherry Pie

(Joe Josea)

(During a Stage Show Jess Conrad Had trouble reaching the high notes so Dickie stood behind the curtains and sang them)

He also sang the high notes on Jess Conrad's record release of Cherry Pie.

Come Softly to Me

(Trevel, Ellis, Christopher)

Sang on Oh Boy Television show, 25th April 1959.

Cool Shake

(Unknown)

Sang on Oh Boy Television show, 25th April 1959.

D

Don't Make Me Love You

(Weisman David)

B Side 45, B Side 45 7" Promo, EP Track, LP Pride Without Prejudice, CD Dickie Pride the Sheik Of Shake, CD Slippin 'n' Slidin With Dickie Pride, CD The Complete Dickie Pride, CD Blood Brothers, CD Three Cool Cats. CD Dickie Pride Slippin and Slidin.CD Dickie Pride the Shiek of Shake.

E

F

Frantic

(May Norman)

A side 45, USA, B Side 45, B Side 45 Germany, B Side 45 Netherlands, B Side 45 Norway, EP Track, LP Pride Without Prejudice, CD Dickie Pride the Sheik Of Shake, CD Slippin 'n' Slidin With Dickie Pride, CD The Complete Dickie Pride, CD Blood Brothers, CD Three Cool Cats. CD Dickie Pride Slippin and Slidin.

Fabulous Cure

Marcus Benjamin)

B Side 45, B Side 45, B Side 45 Demo, EP Track, LP Pride Without Prejudice, CD Dickie Pride The Sheik Of Shake, CD Slippin 'n' Slidin With Dickie Pride, CD The Complete Dickie Pride, CD Blood Brothers, CD Three Cool Cats.CD Dickie Pride The Sheik of Shake

Falling in love

(Chester Mann Dee Henion)

LP Pride Without Prejudice, CD Dickie Pride the Sheik Of Shake, CD Slippin 'n' Slidin With Dickie Pride, CD The Complete Dickie Pride, CD Blood Brothers, CD Three Cool Cats. CD Dickie Pride Slippin and Slidin.CD Dickie Pride the Sheik Of Shake.

G

Give Me the Simple Life

(Bloom Ruby)

LP Pride Without Prejudice, CD Dickie Pride the Sheik of Shake, CD Slippin 'n' Slidin With Dickie Pride, CD The Complete Dickie Pride, CD Blood Brothers, CD Three Cool Cats. CD Dickie Pride Slippin and Slidin CD Dickie Pride the Sheik of Shake.

Get On the Right Track Baby

(Titus Turner)

Was recorded in 1965 onto a demo single and was submitted to Fontana Records but was rejected by their A + R man but is unreleased.

<u>H</u>

<u>I</u>

It's Only a Paper Moon

(Arlen Harburg Rose)

LP Pride Without Prejudice, CD Dickie Pride the Sheik of Shake, CD Slippin 'n' Slidin, With Dickie Pride, CD The Complete Dickie Pride, CD Blood Brothers, CD Three Cool Cats. CD Dickie Pride Slippin and Slidin.CD Dickie Pride the Sheik of Shake.

Isn't this A Lovely Day

(Berlin)

LP Pride Without Prejudice, CD Dickie Pride The Sheik Of Shake, CD Slippin' n Slidin With Dickie Pride, CD The Complete Dickie Pride, CD Blood Brothers, CD Three Cool Cats.CD Dickie Pride The Sheik of Shake.

Isn't It A Lovely Day

(Berlin)

(Was Put Onto Tape By Associated Rediffusion Television For An Audition at Their Kingsway Studios)

I Could Write a Book

(Rodgers and Hart)

LP Pride Without Prejudice, CD Dickie Pride the Sheik Of Shake, CD Slippin 'n' Slidin With Dickie Pride, Cd The Complete Dickie Pride, CD Blood Brothers, CD Three Cool Cats. CD

Dickie Pride Slippin and Slidin.CD Dickie Pride the Shiek of Shake

I Go Ape

(Neil Sedaka, Howard Greenfield)

(Unreleased Demo as Heard On the Dickie Pride Television Program Jukebox Heroes.)

J

K

L

Let's Make a Habit Of This

(Reed)

A Side 45, CD the Complete Dickie Pride, CD Blood Brothers.CD Dickie Pride The Sheik of Shake

Loch Lomond

(Trad Arranged Jupp)

LP Pride Without Prejudice, CD Dickie Pride the Sheik of Shake, CD Slippin 'n' Slidin With Dickie Pride, CD The Complete Dickie Pride, CD Blood Brothers, CD Three Cool Cats. CD Dickie Pride the Sheik of Shake.

Lu Lu's Back in Town

(Warren Burn)

LP Pride Without Prejudice, CD Dickie Pride the Sheik of Shake, CD Slippin 'n' Slidin With Dickie Pride, CD The Complete Dickie Pride, CD Blood Brothers, CD Three Cool Cats. CD Dickie Pride Slippin and Slidin.CD Dickie Pride the Sheik of Shake.

Look Homeward Angel

(Thomas Wolfe)

(Sang in the washroom at The John Newnham Washroom for a Bunch of His Friends)

Long Tall Sally

(Little Richard, Johnson, Blackwell)

Sung on Oh Boy Television Show 25th April 1959.

Little Boy Don't Get Scared

(Jon Hendricks)

(Sang this on the George Melly Jazz Beat Show on BBC Radio)

M

Moody's Mood for Love

(Eddie Jefferson)

(Sang This on the George Melly Jazz Beat Show on BBC Radio)

Midnight Oil

(D Sherman B Sherman)

A Side 45, EP Track, EP Track, LP Pride Without Prejudice, CD Dickie Pride the Sheik of Shake, CD Slippin 'n' Slidin With Dickie Pride, CD The Complete Dickie Pride, CD Blood Brothers, CD Three Cool Cats. CD Dickie Pride Slippin and Slidin.CD Dickie Pride the Sheik of Shake.

<u>N</u>

No John

(Jeffries)

LP Pride Without Prejudice, CD Dickie Pride the Sheik of Shake, CD Slippin 'n' Slidin With Dickie Pride, CD The Complete Dickie Pride, CD Blood Brothers, CD Three Cool Cats. CD Dickie Pride Slippin and Slidin.CD Dickie Pride the Sheik of Shake.

O

Out of Sight

(James Brown)

(Recorded twice once for a Demo

And once for Joe Meek, with a view to releasing it, in 1965).

P

Primrose Lane

(Callender Shanklin)

A Side 45, A Side 45 Germany, A Side 45 Netherlands, A Side 45 Norway, EP Track, LP Pride Without Prejudice, CD Dickie Pride the Sheik of Shake, CD Slippin 'n' Slidin With Dickie Pride, CD The Complete Dickie Pride, CD Blood Brothers, CD Three Cool Cats. CD Dickie Pride Slippin and Slidin.CD Dickie Pride the Sheik of Shake.

Q

R

S

Sack O Woe

(Cannonball Adderley)

(Sang this on the George Melly Jazz Beat Show on BBC Radio)

Sticks And Stones

(Titus Turner)

(Often Sung on Tour)

Slippin 'n' Slidin

(Little Richard, Eddie Bo, Albert Collins)

A Side 45, A Side 45 Promo, A Side 45 Demo, EP Track, EP Track, CD Dickie Pride the Sheik Of Shake, CD Slippin 'n' Slidin With Dickie Pride, CD The Complete Dickie Pride, CD Blood Brothers, CD Three Cool Cats.CD Dickie Pride The Sheik of Shake

Slippin 'n' Slidin

(Little Richard, Eddie Bo, Albert Collins)

Sung an extended Version, on the Oh Boy Television Show 4th April 1959.CD Dickie Pride the Sheik of Shake

Slippin 'n' Slidin

(Little Richard, Eddie Bo, Albert Collins)

Sung a shortened version, on the Oh Boy Television Show 30th May 1959.

Such a Night

(Lincoln Chase)

(Unreleased recorded 1957 onto a demo disc paid for by a group of Richard's Friends)

Also, Dickie stepped in for Danny Rivers on an Appearance on Wham to get the high notes for him.

T

The Little White Cloud That Cried

(Johnny Ray)

(Was sung in the Washroom of the John Newnham School for A Bunch of Richard's Friends.

To Close for Comfort

(Weise Holofcener)

LP Pride Without Prejudice, CD Dickie Pride the Sheik of Shake, CD Slippin 'n' Slidin With Dickie Pride, CD The Complete Dickie Pride, CD Blood Brothers, CD Tree Cool Cats.CD Dickie Pride The Sheik of Shake.

The Kissing Had To Stop

(Johnson)

B Side 45, CD The Complete Dickie Pride, CD Blood Brothers.

They Can't Take That Away from Me

(Gershwin)

LP Pride Without Prejudice, CD Dickie Pride the Sheik of Shake, CD Slippin 'n' Slidin With Dickie Pride, CD The Complete Dickie Pride, CD Blood Brothers, CD Three Cool Cats. CD Dickie Pride Slippin and Slidin. CD Dickie Pride the Sheik of Shake.

There's A Small Hotel

(Rogers and Hart)

LP Pride Without Prejudice, CD Dickie Pride the Sheik of Shake, CD Slippin 'n' Slidin with Dickie Pride, CD The Complete Dickie Pride, CD Blood Brothers, CD Three Cool Cats. CD Dickie Pride Slippin and Slidin.CD Dickie Pride the Sheik of Shake.

There's A Small Hotel

(Roger and Hart)

(A Tape of Dickie Singing This Was Recorded At Associated Rediffusion Television Studios Kingsway for An Audition)

Time and a River

(Thomas Wolfe)

(Sang at Associated Rediffusion Television Kingsway Studios for an Audition and Was Put on Tape)

He also sang it on the Rock n Trad Spectacular, Idols on parade Tour in November 1960.

Three Cool Cats

(Jerry Leiber, Mike Stoller)

Dickie, Cliff Richard and Marty Wilde sung this on the final television show of Oh Boy on 30th May 1959.CD Dickie Pride the Sheik of Shake.

U

V

W

What'd I Say?

(Ray Charles)

(Often Sung on Tour)

Walking the Dog

(Rufus Thomas)

(Dickie Sang This at The Flamingo in 1965)

Walking

(Miles Davis)

(Sang this on the George Melly Jazz Beat Show on BBC radio)

X

Y

You're Singing Our Love Song to Somebody Else

(Shroder Hill B Feldman)

LP Pride Without Prejudice, CD Dickie Pride the Sheik of Shake, CD Slippin 'n' Slidin With Dickie Pride, CD The Complete Dickie Pride, CD Blood Brothers, CD Three Cool Cats. CD Dickie Pride Slippin and Slidin.CD Dickie Pride the Sheik of Shake.

You Turned the Tables on Me

(Mitchell)

LP Pride Without Prejudice, CD Dickie Pride the Sheik of Shake, CD Slippin 'n' Slidin With Dickie Pride, CD The Complete Dickie Pride, CD Blood Brothers, CD Three Cool Cats.CD Dickie Pride Slippin and Slidin.CD Dickie Pride The Sheik of Shake.

Z

Dickie on Film

Dickie can be seen on the two surviving tapes of Television's Oh Boy Show,

4th April 1959 he can be seen singing an extended version of Slippin' n Slidin.

30th May 1959 the Last Show, he can be seen singing a shortened version of Slippin 'n' Slidin.

He can also be seen singing Three Cool Cats with Marty Wilde, Cliff Richard and Dickie.

There is a 30-minute Tribute/Documentary

That was shown on BBC television in July 2002 Called Jukebox Heroes'... Dickie Pride.

Featured on the show were rare tracks including 'I Go Ape'.

Billy Fury

Billy Fury was Dickie's best friend, and they shared a bond of friendship between them, so deep that they become 'Blood brothers'.

Bill Fury was born Ronald Wycherley at the Smith down Infirmary in Liverpool, on April the 17th 1940.

Like all boys born in the years of the war he was mischievous but a normal boy.

At the age of Six Ronnie contracted Rheumatic fever this was to leave him with week heart valves.

When Ronnie was fourteen, he received his first guitar

After working in a job that he didn't like he settled down to working on a tugboat called the Formby, it was while he worked on this boat he was able to write some of his music, among the songs he wrote was a song called 'Collette' later to become one of his hits, he and a few friends from the boat used to perform as the skiffle group 'the Formby Skiffle Group' in the local café's and working men's clubs

By this time Ronnie was a teddy boy, with crepe shoes and drape jacket, all was going well until he transferred from The Formby to another tug, he had an argument with the skipper and punched him in the mouth.

After appearing in a talent contest in 1957 Ronnie decided that his future lay in his music so with a change of name to Stean Wade, he went into a recording booth and recorded himself a demo Disc with an objective of sending to producers.

It was decided that he would instead send a real-to-real tape to impresario Larry Parnes who toured the country with package shows of various acts.

Parnes invited Ronnie to meet him the next time he was in the area,

 Which was at the Essoldo, Birkenhead on October the 1st 1958, Marty Wilde was topping the bill.

Vince Eager and Dougie Wright (John Barry's Drummer) were going for a wimpy Burger, when they got outside of the stage door, there stood a James Dean look-alike with the collar of his raincoat turned up, looking very moody.

he asked if Larry Parnes was about as he had sent him a tape of songs he had written and he wanted to know if he liked them, he was hoping to sell a couple of his songs to Marty Wilde.

When he met Larry, he was asked to play a couple of his songs, he borrowed a guitar and played 'Maybe Tomorrow'. Everyone was gob smacked as no one wrote their own music in those days he was asked to play something else, and 'Margo' was played. it was then suggested by Larry that he should go on, he went on, he was introduced as one of their own 'Stean Wade' , Larry had to push him through the curtains, but his performance stole the show that night.

By the time Parnes' show arrived at its next destination Ronnie was signed and repackaged as Billy Fury.

Not long after that Billy met Dickie Pride, and they were to become lifelong friends

Billy's personal stage act was defined, and it was dynamite.

Mark Crossways of 'Picture' magazine wrote of Billy's Performance.

"Many teenage girls work themselves into a state of frenzy when watching Fury's actions on Stage, the cause was one number in Fury's act on an Elvis Presley original called 'Mean Woman Blue's' Fury twists his mouth into a vicious shape, and glares into the spotlight, he looks defiant,

Slowly to the throb of guitars he sings the opening bars, then with deliberate calculation he winds his leg around the microphone, he has developed his technique. he knew the exact moment to leap back from the microphone, his next move increases the tension among the female element of his audience, with hunched shoulders and an agonizing expression he undoes the zip of his yellow jacket, down it comes,

While the screams increase in volume, with a swift movement he casts the jacket aside and grabs hold of the microphone.

His previous exhibition seems tame in the light of what follows, over goes the microphone with fury on top of it".

By April 1959 Billy had signed a seven-year contract with Decca Records, he was also appearing in a television play called 'Strictly for Sparrows' on the show he was to perform a bit of a song in the background, but the producers were so impressed he sang a complete song, he sang the self-penned song 'Maybe Tomorrow' which was to catapult him into the charts, it reached number 18

The B side was another self-penned song 'Gonna Type A Letter'.

He was now hot property, and he appeared on various tours for Parnes and Television shows including the number one teen show 'Oh Boy'.

By 1960 he had his first top ten hit with another self-penned hit 'Collette'

By now his stage act was being frowned upon as being too raunchy.

In April 1960 he appeared on the tour with the legendary Eddie Cochran and Gene Vincent.

He also appeared at Great Yarmouth with Marty Wilde, Johnny Gentle, Duffy Power and Dickie

Pride, by this time Billy and Dickie were the best of friends and were inseparable.

Billy Fury's legendary ten-inch album 'The Sound of Fury' was released, this iconic album is considered the best rockabilly album to come out of England, Joe Brown was the guitarist on the album, the album reached number 18 in the album charts, no mean feat for a totally self-penned album.

After the album, Billy was to receive an image change; he was to be presented as an all-round entertainer.

His next two singles 'A Thousand Stars' and 'Don't Worry' only helped to reinforce the idea that he was now a ballad singer.

His next hit became Billy's best loved song it was 'Halfway to Paradise,' it entered the charts in May and stayed there for 24 weeks, eventually reaching number 3 in the pop charts earning him his first silver disc.

It was at this time that Billy intervened several times to stop Dickie Pride being fired by Larry Parnes who wanted to drop him.

He met Ivor Raymonde the arranger this partnership was very successful and led to 11 top 20 hits over the next three years.

In September 1961, Billy's most successful single to date was released; it was a cover of Frankie Laine's 'Jealousy' this reached number 2 in the singles chart.

Still touring, his popularity was second to none; he was booked up to eighteen months in advance and had a reputation for completing songs in the studio after only one take.

he released two more albums over the next few months 'Billy Fury' and 'Halfway to Paradise', he was voted number three in the top ten of male singers in 1961 but in 1962 he was voted number 2 after Cliff Richard.

he was still touring and decided that he now needed a permanent backing band, so he returned to Liverpool to hold auditions, he rejected Gerry and the Pacemakers, Cass and the Casanovas and The Silver Beatles who won the auditions but only if they dropped the bass player Stuart Sutcliffe who performed as if he had no interest and kept his back to the audience, they refused.

finally he recruited the Tornadoes who were to appear in Billy's next project a movie called 'Play it Cool' it wasn't great but it was ok, but the Ep soundtrack was highly successful staying in the charts for 45 weeks it got to number 2, because of its release at school holiday time it was a great success, it played to packed houses up and down the country, at the end of filming though Billy collapsed with Bronchitis and he was hospitalized for three weeks, this is when he found out that his health was going to be a problem to him.

Billy's fourth album was released it was simply called 'Billy'; it was a massive hit and was a second top ten album for Billy.

In April 1962 Billy was taken to America by Larry Parnes for a short holiday, while there he met his idol Elvis Presley on the set of Girls, Girls, Girls, and he presented him with two silver discs, Elvis thought that Billy was a swell guy and Billy thought that Elvis was a humble and friendly guy and added that he moved like an animal, real cool.

When Billy returned to England he recorded 'Because Of love' the same version as was in the film.

Over the next few months, he had two number 3 hits with 'like I've Never Been Gone' and 'When Will You Say I Love You'

He was so popular at this time that Billy Fury monthly was released; it was so popular that it lasted four years.

in November 1963 his luck nearly ran out he nearly became another road statistic when he and Dickie Pride had a car accident in Billy's ford Zephyr which ploughed into a pile up on the M1, in all fifteen cars were involved, Billy suffered concussion and a broken arm.

Mrs. C A Johnson takes up the story "I remember queuing for tickets to see Billy Fury in the big Star show with my friend, and I got two tickets for the front row at the Rialto in York, in the week he was to appear he had an accident and broke his arm, but the show went on and he appeared with his arm in a sling, he couldn't play guitar, dance or anything, he just came on stage sang a few songs, took a bow and went, that was the only time I saw him in person, he was wonderful".

During 1963 and 1964 he released hit record after hit record, one of them was his best LP to date (personal opinion) 'We Want Billy' it was an attempt to capture Billy's live performance, it was only 31 minutes long, but it was fantastic.

During 1964 he had his last top five single called 'In Summer', by this time 'the Tornado's had gone their separate ways, and Billy held a press conference to introduce his new band the 'Gamblers'.

they joined Billy in his new summer show that was to last three and a half months at the Royal Aquarium theatre in Great Yarmouth, while there he filmed his next movie 'I've Got A Horse' this was a dire movie built around his love of animals, in fact on of the tracks on the movie was called 'I Love Animals'.

The Gamblers joined Billy on a lengthy autumn tour, Billy was ill during some of these dates and Dickie Pride used to cover for him by going on instead of Billy.

When the Beatles were dominating the charts both here and in America, Billy was still churning out hit after hit, matching anything that the beat boom could throw at him.

In 1966 Billy recorded his last single for Decca Records 'Give Me Your Word' which reached a respectable number 7.

He also won Radio Luxembourg top artist and in 1967 he signed with his new label Parlophone where he had 11 singles in three years, the first was 'Hurting Is Loving', the next few singles though good releases, didn't chart.

Mainly to do with his bad health he was unable to go on the road to promote them.

Even though Billy's health was preventing him from touring, it didn't stop him from using the studio.

at the end of 1968 Billy was to see Dickie Pride again, when they bumped into each other in a Croydon Street they were to have a meal together, both Billy and Dickie were both very ill men at this time, and it showed.

He spent more and more time in hospital and recuperated at his farm in Wales

In 1969 Billy married his then girlfriend Judith Hall, but this marriage ended in divorce, Billy admitted that it was a mistake from the start.

In December 1971 Billy underwent open heart surgery for a valve that was not working properly.

in 1972 Billy set up the Fury record label that released singles by Shane Fenton, Johnny Hacket and by this time one of his own singles 'Will the Real Man Please Stand Up' which was well received.

by 1973 he had kept his good looks and did a cameo appearance in David Essex's film 'That'll Be the Day', he sang five classic rock and roll numbers, and the album was a best seller reaching number one in the album charts.

As Stormy tempest, resident rocker of a holiday camp, his part was brief but very memorable. when Jim MacLaine (David Essex) asks Stormy's drummer (Keith Moon) if the songs were his own the answer was swift:" You have to be American to write Rock and Roll" if Billy Fury, Britain's only true Rock and Roller was listening he must have winced considering his output as Billy Fury, Ron Wycherley and Wilbur Wilberforce.

In June 1974 his last single for the next seven years was released on the Warner Brothers label the A side was produced by his old friend Marty Wilde 'I'll Be Your Sweetheart' and the B side 'Fascinating Candle Flame' was written by Billy Fury.

He was now semi-retired he did the occasional guest shot over the next couple of years until in 1976 he again underwent open heart surgery.

He was by now retired and was spending most of his time at his farm in Wales with his animals, but this was to be short lived,

In 1978 he was presented with a massive tax bill of £ 16 000 left over from his days working with Larry Parnes, he was furious with Parnes, and he never forgave him,

Although he was ill, he turned up at the bankruptcy court,

But a lifeline was thrown to him, by Ktel records they wanted him to record an album of his old hits, for this they would pay off his debts and give him royalties, Billy was given an immediate discharge.

Late in 1978 he recorded the album for Ktel entitled 'The Golden Years' it was as promised a rerecording of all of his old hits.

For the next couple of years, he did the odd gig around the country but spent most of his spare time at his farm.

In 1980 he appeared on the Stuart Henry MS Appeal concert where he sang 'Wondrous Place'.

by 1981 he was feeling much better well enough to appear at the Elvis Presley fan club convention in London, he was the man who had come closest to Elvis in their affection, and he was there in person, one thousand Elvis fans gave him the loudest, foot stomping ovation ever given to a man, by the most loyal Elvis fans in the world.

By the end of 1981 Billy's confidence had returned, he signed with Polydor records, his first single 'Be Mine Tonight' followed by 'Love or Money' both reached the charts,

He appeared on The Russell Harty television show, and he sang his next single 'Devil or Angel',

He did various local radio shows and interviews to promote the single, all was going well until he collapsed at his farm suffering from partial paralysis and temporary blindness,

his girlfriend Lisa Rosen drove him to a London hospital, the doctors did not hold much hope, but he pulled through, making a complete recovery.

In 1982 he embarked on a comeback tour up and down the country, the 'sound of Fury' was reissued by Decca and Billy had a new single out, a live version of 'Wondrous Place'.

1983 started off with a promise, he recorded six tracks for the television show unforgettable, and he was in the studio producing for a new female singer he had discovered, called Ricky O, he often worked late in the studio.

On the 27th of January 1983 Billy was working late in the studio, he returned home to his flat and Lisa in St John's wood. The next morning Lisa went out and left Billy sleeping,

When his manager Tony Reid went to pick him up that morning he couldn't wake him, he called an ambulance that rushed Billy to St Mary's hospital, but Billy was pronounced dead on arrival at 12-10 pm.

He was the same age as his idol, Elvis Presley he was 42.

Media coverage was extensive, tributes poured in from friends in the music business, family and friends alike.

Both Polydor and Decca released best of albums and a fan club was set up by Tony Reid.

Billy fury may have been known as the second Elvis, but this is untrue he was The One and Only Billy Fury.

Billy Fury Discography

Decca

Maybe Tomorrow / gonna type a letter	59
Margo / don't knock upon my door	59
Angel Face / Time has come	59
My Christmas prayer / Last Kiss	59
Collette / Baby How I cried	60
That's love / you don't Know	60
Wondrous place / allright goodbye	60
A thousand stars / Push Push	60
Don't worry / Talking in my sleep	61
Halfway to paradise / Cross my heart	61
Jealousy / Open your arms	61
I'd never find another you / Sleepless nights	61
Letter full of tears / Magic Eyes	62
Last night was made for love / A King for tonight	62
Once upon a dream / if I lose you	62
Because of love / Running around	62
Like I've never been gone / what do you think you're doing of	63

When will you say I love you/ all I wanna do is cry   63

In summer / I'll never fall in love again   63

Somebody else's girl /go ahead and ask her   63

Do you really love me too /what am I gonna do   63

I will / Nothin Shakin (but the leaves on the tree   64

It's only make believe / baby what do you want   64

I'm lost without you / you better believe it baby   65

In thoughts of you / away from you   65

Run to my loving arms / where do you run   65

I'll never quite get over you / I belong to the wind   66

Don't let a little pride / didn't see the real thing come along   66

Give me your word / she's so far out she's in   66

Parlophone

 Hurting is loving / things are changing   67

Loving you / I'll go along with it   67

Suzanne in the mirror it just don't matter now 67

Beyond the shadow of a doubt / baby do you love me 67

Silly boy blue / one minute woman 68

Phone box / any morning now 68

Lady / certain things 68

I call for my rose /bye bye 69

All the way to the USA /do my best for you 69

Why are you leaving /old roll (hi de hi) 70

Paradise alley / well alright 70

Fury

Will the real man please stand up /at this stage 72

Warner Brothers

I'll be your sweetheart / fascinating candle flame 74

Nems

Halfway to paradise / turn my back on you 76

Decca

Jealousy / last night was made for love 78

Don't knock upon my door / Margo 79

Gonna type a letter /maybe tomorrow	79

Polydor

Be mine tonight / no trespassers	81
Love or money love sweet love	82
Devil or angel / don't tell me lies	82
Forget him / your words	83
Let me go lover / your words	83

Old Gold

Halfway to paradise / last night was made for love	83
Jealousy / I will	91

EP's

Decca

1 Maybe tomorrow	59
2. Billy Fury	61
3. Billy Fury no 2	62
4. Play it cool	62
5, Billy Fury Hits	62
6. Billy Fury and the Tornados	63
7. Am I blue	63

8. Billy Fury and the gamblers	65
9. My Christmas Prayer	83

Magnum Force

10. Suzanne in the mirror	85

LP's

Decca

1. The Sound of fury	60

Ace of clubs

2. Billy Fury	60
3. Halfway to paradise	61

Decca

4. We Want Billy	63
5. Billy	63

K Tel

6. Memories	83

Polydor

7. The one and only	83

Magnum Force

8. Sticks and stones	85

K Tel

9. The Best Of   89

Larry Parnes

Larry Parnes was the most famous manager of the 1950's he was a born entrepreneur.

Larry Parnes was born in Willesden, London in 1930, Laurence Maurice Parnes.

He proved his entrepreneurial skills from an early age when he produced his first show when he was just eight years old featuring child stars.

He left school when he was sixteen and worked for his family clothing business,

 By the time he was eighteen he had three ladies' clothes shops of his own, only one was a success.

by the mid 50's he was looking around for new opportunities, when a friend took him to a bar called 'La Caverne' in the west end.

 Where at the end of the evening he managed to calm down an argument between the two owners,

The upshot being that by the end of that evening Larry owned half of the bar,

As one of them was willing to sell up rather than work with the other, it cost Larry £500, paid in instalments.

It was 1955 and the cliental of the bar were select, mainly because of the ladder that had to be climbed to get into the place, there were no stairs.

Larry, who was tee total at this time, started to drink whiskey.

One Day a joker decided to challenge him to a Whiskey drinking contest, within half an hour he was drunk, his co-owner found him in the theatrical district and took him home to sleep it off.

The next day there was a knock on the door, a man had come to him to talk to him about 'The Play', and during the last evenings drinking he had agreed to produce a play called 'The House of Shame'

Larry had agreed to invest in the play, paying in instalments.

the play toured the country in 1955 but did not do too well, but when he recruited publicist John Kennedy who changed the title of the play to a sleazier title to 'Women of The Streets' along with two actresses hired to stand outside dressed as prostitutes,

When the actresses were arrested as real prostitutes

The resulting publicity was sensational, before long the play was making a profit.

a chance meeting with John Kennedy at the 'Sabrina' coffee bar in Soho led to Larry's encounter with a young lad called Tommy Hicks at 'the Stork Club' in Regents Street, by the end of the evening Hicks had asked the two of them to be his manager.

Parnes had promised to make him a star in three months, if not he would tear up his contract.

With a name change to Tommy Steele he was to maintain a clean wholesome image,

Within six weeks Tommy was England's first Rock and Roll star.

With a newly signed record contract with Decca

He released his first single 'Rock with the Caveman'.

With television shows and stage appearances under his belt Steele could do no wrong and nor could impresario Larry Parnes,

With a bit of polish Tommy was promoted as an all-round entertainer.

Tommy Steele starred in movies and by 1960 he was indeed a family entertainer that you could take your kids to see.

Larry was now a great believer in Rock and Roll, and he was very impressed by the technology of the day, the television industry of 1956 was an ideal way for him to get into traditional show business.

it all came to a head with Tommy Steele though when he announced his engagement,

The teenagers of the day didn't want their Rock and Roll stars getting married,

This was the end as far as his Rock and Roll days were concerned.

In 1957 Parnes tried to recreate the glory days with Tommy's younger brother Colin Hicks, but they were unsuccessful, after this Kennedy split with Parnes and left show business.

He had had enough.

Parnes though wanted more of the same, Lionel Bart who co-wrote some of Tommy Steele's hits took Parnes to see a young man that he had just seen at the Condor club Reg Smith, but he had just left,

Because of Bart's enthusiasm for the lad Parnes went round to his house and signed him there on the spot.

Parnes groomed his new star and even gave him a new name Marty Wilde, which he hated, so they tossed a coin to see if he kept the name or not Reg lost.

He has since said that he thought about it and was now in agreement with Larry, Marty Wilde is a fantastic rock n roll name.

During 1957, with a new name and a recording contract with Phillips he was plugged extensively but never charted.

By 1958 Marty Wilde was Britain's most famous Rock and roll star.

Lucrative television contracts with 6.5 Special eventually cast him into the public eye and by June he hit the charts with 'Endless Sleep'.

Larry Parnes had made a lot of Show business contacts over the last few years, and he was able to get work for his talented stars because of these contacts.

When Jack Good moved to independent television, Parnes negotiated for Marty Wilde to be his resident star on the show 'Oh Boy', all went well until a month later when Jack Good's own discovery Cliff Richard hit the show in direct competition to Marty Wilde, Parnes was furious, and he dragged Marty Wilde physically from the show's rehearsals. But by December things were smoothed over and Marty was back on the show.

Larry explains:

"I knew Jacks temperament; I did blow my top and I regretted it because I had no desire to upset Jack or Marty.

But I did have an arrangement whereby Marty would be the star of 'Oh Boy' and I objected strongly that someone else was going to be brought in…

That was loyalty to my artiste. I think Jack recognized that… I had a great respect for Jack Good and if I hadn't Marty would not have been back on 'Oh Boy''.

Marty like Tommy Steele finished his Rock and roll career in 1959 by announcing that he was engaged and was going to marry Joyce Baker a Vernon's girl.

By 1963 after an unsuccessful few years trying to sing Rock and roll and trying his hand at ballads, and the dawning of the Mersey beat era Marty left Parnes' management.

in 1958 Parnes' third discovery was Vince Eager (Roy Taylor) he was a hard-working dedicated performer, he became a minor star of 'Oh Boy' and became a household name on the BBC's program 'Drumbeat'.

Eager left Parnes after a disagreement about his contract with Parnes, he left to be managed by his brother-in-law, this was a disaster and his career collapsed without Parnes,

Who knows how famous he might have become, to be fair to Vince Eager he was good, good enough to carve a career of his own and he is still performing today in 2020

In 1958 Parnes met his greatest discovery, Ronald Wycherley, whom he met at the Essoldo cinema in Birkenhead, at a show Marty, was headlining,

Parnes was so impressed by Ron that he was put on that very night and a contract was signed the very next day.

So, with a new name enter Billy Fury.

Within weeks Billy had successfully auditioned for a television play called 'Strictly for Sparrows' he had a recording contract with Decca records, and he went on 'Oh Boy'.

By the end of the decade Larry Parnes had increased his roster of stars or as the press had dubbed them his 'Stable of Stars' or his boys,

Larry Parnes:

"They go through a very extensive grooming. It is sometimes five months before they appear on stage or three months before I let them do any recording,

To start with, they have physical grooming. I have their hair cut- this is very important. Sometimes, they may have bad skin which has to be attended to. Then I get them suitable clothes and provide them with comfort

. I like them to have a touch of luxury from the start so that if they make the big time, they don't lose their heads. I like them to live in a good home; get three good meals a day go to bed early and have plenty of fresh air."

Parnes Blitzed the country with Parnes' talent on package tours, they were to include Dickie Pride (Richard Kneller) Duffy Power (Ray Howard), Johnny Gentle (John Askew), Terry Dene, Nelson Keene, Peter Wynne, Georgie fame (Clive Powell), and Joe Brown, whom Parnes wanted to call Elmer Twitch there was even a girl, called Sally Kelly.

Larry Believed in all of his boys, sending them on exhausting tours of one night stands up and down the country and all his boys worked exclusively through him in fact he was so good at his job promoting his boys that he could fill a hall using his name alone, punters knew that they would get value for money, his contracts at best were 60/40 in his favour and he kept his boys on wages paying them if they were working or not so you could bet your life they would be working, he had a reputation for being mean with his money and he often gave his boys return train tickets to gigs.

He even tried to work with the disgraced Terry Dene, but his comeback was short lived, he eventually disappeared.

by 1960 the press were calling him 'Mr. Parnes, Shillings and Pence, which conveyed his shrewdness as a manager, but this gave the idea that he was only interested in money, this was a distortion of the truth, if anything he was too generous but too overprotective and manipulative, but he was not a con man (he was really) he was a businessman.

by the early 1960's he was the most famous impresario in England, his package tours covered most of the country and had the biggest names in show business at that time on them, his shows were selling out never more so than in 1960 when the Parnes package tours were to play host to Gene Vincent and Eddie Cochran.

In 1960 there was a turning of the tide when he got together with Allan Williams a promoter of Liverpool groups.

Larry needed a backing band for Billy Fury, so Parnes had Williams set up auditions, among those auditioned were the Silver Beatles, he didn't sign them that day, but he did have them do a two week engagement of Scotland with Johnny Gentle.

Larry had another chance to sign them in 1962, but he didn't, by this time he was bored of the music industry and he decided to wind down his Stable of acts in order to pursue a career in the theatre his transition was successful,

by 1967 he was unable to manage Billy Fury so a ten year relationship came to an end in 1968 he put on a play about homosexuality in a Canadian prison he lost a small fortune.

In 1972 he bought a twelve-year lease of the Cambridge theatre, and he put on two musicals, Chicago and Charlie girl, and he administered the business affairs of international ice skater John Curry during the rest of the 1970's.

In 1981 he developed meningitis, and he retired completely.

He died of pneumonia in 1989 at his home.

Parnes' Stable of Stars or Larry's boys were

Tommy Steele, (Tommy Hicks)

Marty Wilde (Reginald Smith)

Vince Eager (Roy Taylor)

Billy Fury (Ronald Wycherley)

Dickie Pride (Richard Kneller)

Lance Fortune (Chris Morris)

Duffy Power (Ray Howard)

Johnny Gentle (John Askew)

Terry Dene (Terence Williams)

Nelson Keene (Malcolm Holland)

Georgie Fame (Clive Powell)

Julian X (Julian Scott)

Colin Hicks, Tommy Bruce, Joe Brown, Peter Wynne, Davy Jones,

 and Sally Kelly the only female in the bunch

He Steered Clear of groups but he did have a few they were

The Tornados,

The Viscounts,

Cabin Boys

And the Silver Beetles and a few others on his tours.

He Also Gave Breaks to Jimmy Tarbuck, Rolf Harris, Des O Connor and Mike Yarwood.

Duffy Power

Duffy Power was one of Dickie Pride's closest friends for a while, they stayed friends right up to the end and if Dickie had not died it was quite likely that they would have worked together again either as an act on the same bill or collaborating on song writing.

Duffy Power was born in Fulham London in 1941. His name was Ray Howard

In 1959 when Ray was seventeen, he was working in a laundry,

It was while he was working in the Laundry that he entered a jive contest at his local Saturday morning teenage show, in the audience was impresario Larry Parnes who had went along to see a local band with a mind to signing them.

When Ray sang Parnes was so impressed by his voice and his energy that he signed him up.

So with a new name of Duffy Power, he was now a member of that exclusive club of Parnes' stable of stars, Parnes' golden boys,

Duffy's stage performances were dynamite, he used to dress in a gold lame suit,

But his chart success was limited as Parnes couldn't spot a hit record for him.

He made Duffy record second hand American tracks.

it was not only Duffy though but nearly all of his acts.

it was during this time that Duffy met Dickie Pride and Billy Fury, the three of them became firm friends they were even to share a flat together.

Duffy became disillusioned with Parnes' management and thought that he was never going to make it under his management, so he parted company with him in late 1961.

He appeared on 'Ready Steady Go'

things did not go well, and the bookings became less and less, it was in 1961 that Duffy became so desperate that he tried to gas himself, only to be rescued by a friend, this friend took him to a blues club to cheer him up, it was while he was at the club he decided that this was the music for him.

In 1963 he had teamed up with Ginger Baker and Jack Bruce and John McLaughlin to form the Graham Bond Quartet.

Their version of the Beatles' 'I Saw Her Standing there, 'with Duffy on lead vocals, is a milestone in blues music.

In 1965 he was now dependant on drugs and spent some more time with Dickie Pride who was also dependant on drugs.

Duffy appeared on various albums with Alexis corners blues incorporated, including 'Red hot from Alex in 1964,

Sky high in 1966 and blues incorporated in 1967,

But by 1968 the work had dried up and Duffy was out of work

By this time Duffy was in the grip of barbiturates and was suffering from a mental illness, he became reclusive and spent most of his time alone writing songs in his flat.

Between 1968 and 1973 he recorded for the BBC.

Some of these sessions were The John Peel show and the Mike Raven radio1 show

by the early 1970's he was making a slow but steady recovery and started to work as a session's musician

And he played on the soundtrack of the smash hit movie the Italian job,

In 1971 he recorded an album; this has come to be known as the lost album, as it was never released.

in the 1980's he was well enough to record again and put down some of the songs that he wrote while he was alone in his flat,

they became classics,

In 1992 a compilation of his blues, R and B and his rock songs was released to a new generation of listeners, The album was called 'Blues Power' on the See for Miles label

In 2003 an album called 'Just Stay Blue' was released and some of the missing tracks from the lost album were released on it.

Also, in 2003 he recorded a song for a special compilation album

The album was called the Wildlife album; the song was called 'Sweet Again'

Today Duffy Power is considered a pioneer of the blues in this country and more and more listeners are turning to his music.

It could be argued that he is probably one of the most successful of all of Parnes' boys today.

Duffy Power died suddenly on the nineteenth of February 2014 aged 72 after a short illness.

Duffy Power Discography

That's my little Suzie /   Dream Lover

1959

Kissing Time / Ain't She sweet

1959

Starry Eyed / Better than you

1959

Whole lotta Shakin going on, if I can dream

1960

I've got nobody/ when we're walking close

1961

No other love / what now

1961

It Ain't necessarily so / if I get lucky someday

1963

Duffy power with the Graham Bond quartet

I saw her standing there /Farewell baby

1963

Hey Girl / woman made trouble

1963

Tired, broke and busted / Parchman Farm

1964

Where am I / I don't care

1964

Duffy's Nucleus

Davy O Brian (Leave that baby alone / July Tree
1967

Hell Hound / Hummingbird
1970

Hummingbird / hell hound
 1971

River / Little Soldiers
1973

Liberation / Song about Jesus
1973

EP The Big Beat
1

Bibliography

Rogan, Johnny, *Starmakers and Svengalis*,Futura Publications,1989.

Leigh,Spencer,*Halfway to Paradise, Britpop, 1955-1962*,Finbarr International,1996.

Higham,Darrel, Mundy, Julie ,*Don't forget me, the Eddie Cochran Story,* Mainstream Publishing Company, 2002

Leigh,Spencer,*Wondrous Face the Billy Fury story*,Finbarr International,2005.

Lowes, Stuart, *The Billy Fury Discography,* Print on Demand, 2017.

Acknowledgements

With thanks to Duffy Power,

 Ann Parsons, (Dickie's sister), Heidi Parsons (Dickies niece) Joe Brown, Alan Wheeler, Hal Carter, Trevor Ure, Paul Pierrot, the BBC, ,my son Stuart Lowes and Daughters Collette Lowes, and   Rebecca Lowes, Mrs J Barrell, Mrs C Fey, Patricia Ludt (Dickies Ex Wife), Mandy Atkinson(Dickie's Girlfriend), Mrs J Wiltshire, Mrs Ure,, Mrs G Gibb, ,Dave Beale, Rockin Ray Mills, Boz Burrell, Noel Gay, Margaret Alderton, Dorothy Orr, Penelope Sutherland Young,   Doreen M Evans, Roy Greenslade, Derek G Arthurs, Brian Bentley. Brian Fowler Vince Eager, Georgie Fame, Marty Wilde, for all their help in researching, my wife Tina, for putting up with. Dickie Pride this. Dickie Pride that. And for inspiring me to write this book in the first place, and especially thanks to Charles Langley, without his valuable help I may not have finished the book, and the invaluable help of Duffy Power. Thank you.

And a big thank you to anyone else that I may have failed to mention, sorry, but thank you.

With Billy Fury

Dickie with Trisha

With Bobbie Shafto & Nelson Keene, the Guv'nors

With the Sidewinders 1966 the pictures of Dickie with a beard performing on stage they are the last known pictures of Dickie they were taken at the twisted Wheel, Manchester.

A POP SINGER IS TOLD: GET A JOB

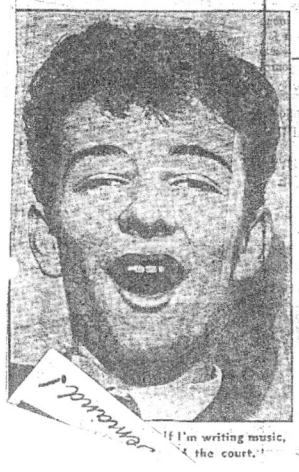

POP and ballad singer Dickie Pride was told yesterday that it was time he found a job.

'Dickie Pride lives on Mum'

He lives at home with his mother.

And SHE has to go out to work to keep him, the magistrates heard at Croydon, London.

Nineteen-year-old Pride — real name Richard Charles Kneller — stood before them accused of a breach of probation.

Not regular

He had been put on probation for three years at West Kent quarter sessions in 1959 for attempted shopbreaking and taking and driving away a vehicle.

But he had failed to lead an industrious life and he had not reported regularly to his probation officer, the court was told.

In December, 1960, he had a disagreement with his agent and his contract was ended.

Royalties

"Since then he has not worked regularly and has been attached to some agency in London," said Mr. P. A. Seal the probation officer. "His contracts have been few and far between."

Kneller, of Healthfield avenue, South Croydon, told the court that he had not had any income during the last five weeks.

"But I might have sold 25,000 records. I don't know. I get paid royalties quarterly.

He said he HAD been working.

"If I am sitting down writing a piece of music, then I am working," he added.

"Some people compose music and get nothing for about twenty years."

'Up to you'

Mr. H. Needham, the chairman, told him: "Everyone in this country has got to keep himself.

"And he doesn't eat if he doesn't earn the money.

"It is up to you to find a job that will bring you a weekly wage—even if it is not in the theatre."

"If I'm writing music, the court."

Billy Fury   Dickie Pride

WANTED

Any information that you can give me about the late great Dickie Pride i.e. Richard Kneller, I am interested in anything, Stories, Anecdotes, Letters, Photographs, Newspaper articles, Sheet Music, written music, demo's Records Recordings, Photographs of records, Albums, EP'S anything, I am hoping to rewrite this book with more information and more visuals about Dickie Pride, do you have any of Dickie's contacts i.e. Friends, Family, people he worked, with Managers agents etc.

If you can help me in any way, please get in touch with me the author Stuart Lowes

No 2 Knella Road.

Welwyn Garden City

Herts

AL7 3NZ

Or E Mail me on:

Lowesstuart2@gmail.com

Also Wanted any information on Larry Parnes and his Stable of stars I am interested in writing a book about them and I am interested in any information to do with them and would be grateful for any information concerning them such as Billy Fury, Nelson Keene, Johnny Gentle, Marty Wilde, Joe Brown, Duffy Power, Georgie Fame, Sally Kelly, Vince Eager, Julian X Terry Dene, Peter Wynne or anyone else that was a Larry Parnes Protégé and of course any information on Parnes himself, His Tours His Professional Life, His Private Life, anyone who knew him and worked with him etc. at the same address as above.

Thank You for all of your help.